ALL

HIS

(A Nicky Lyons FBI Suspense Thriller—Book Two)

BLAKE PIERCE

Blake Pierce

Blake Pierce is the USA Today bestselling author of the RILEY PAGE mystery series, which includes seventeen books. Blake Pierce is also the author of the MACKENZIE WHITE mystery series, comprising fourteen books; of the AVERY BLACK mystery series, comprising six books; of the KERI LOCKE mystery series, comprising five books; of the MAKING OF RILEY PAIGE mystery series, comprising six books; of the KATE WISE mystery series, comprising seven books; of the CHLOE FINE psychological suspense mystery, comprising six books; of the JESSIE HUNT psychological suspense thriller series, comprising twenty six books; of the AU PAIR psychological suspense thriller series, comprising three books; of the ZOE PRIME mystery series, comprising six books; of the ADELE SHARP mystery series, comprising sixteen books, of the EUROPEAN VOYAGE cozy mystery series, comprising six books; of the LAURA FROST FBI suspense thriller, comprising eleven books; of the ELLA DARK FBI suspense thriller, comprising fourteen books (and counting); of the A YEAR IN EUROPE cozy mystery series, comprising nine books, of the AVA GOLD mystery series, comprising six books (and counting); of the RACHEL GIFT mystery series, comprising ten books (and counting); of the VALERIE LAW mystery series, comprising nine books (and counting); of the PAIGE KING mystery series, comprising eight books (and counting); of the MAY MOORE mystery series, comprising eleven books (and counting); the CORA SHIELDS mystery series, comprising five books (and counting); of the NICKY LYONS mystery series, comprising five books (and counting), and of the new CAMI LARK mystery series, comprising five books (and counting).

An avid reader and lifelong fan of the mystery and thriller genres, Blake loves to hear from you, so please feel free to visit www.blakepierceauthor.com to learn more and stay in touch.

THE GIRL HE TOOK (Book #3)
THE GIRL HE WISHED (Book #4)
THE GIRL HE CROWNED (Book #5)
THE GIRL HE WATCHED (Book #6)
THE GIRL HE WANTED (Book #7)
THE GIRL HE CLAIMED (Book #8)

VALERIE LAW MYSTERY SERIES
NO MERCY (Book #1)
NO PITY (Book #2)
NO FEAR (Book #3)
NO SLEEP (Book #4)
NO QUARTER (Book #5)
NO CHANCE (Book #6)
NO REFUGE (Book #7)
NO GRACE (Book #8)
NO ESCAPE (Book #9)

RACHEL GIFT MYSTERY SERIES
HER LAST WISH (Book #1)
HER LAST CHANCE (Book #2)
HER LAST HOPE (Book #3)
HER LAST FEAR (Book #4)
HER LAST CHOICE (Book #5)
HER LAST BREATH (Book #6)
HER LAST MISTAKE (Book #7)
HER LAST DESIRE (Book #8)
HER LAST REGRET (Book #9)
HER LAST HOUR (Book #10)

AVA GOLD MYSTERY SERIES
CITY OF PREY (Book #1)
CITY OF FEAR (Book #2)
CITY OF BONES (Book #3)
CITY OF GHOSTS (Book #4)
CITY OF DEATH (Book #5)
CITY OF VICE (Book #6)

A YEAR IN EUROPE
A MURDER IN PARIS (Book #1)
DEATH IN FLORENCE (Book #2)

VENGEANCE IN VIENNA (Book #3)
A FATALITY IN SPAIN (Book #4)

ELLA DARK FBI SUSPENSE THRILLER
GIRL, ALONE (Book #1)
GIRL, TAKEN (Book #2)
GIRL, HUNTED (Book #3)
GIRL, SILENCED (Book #4)
GIRL, VANISHED (Book 5)
GIRL ERASED (Book #6)
GIRL, FORSAKEN (Book #7)
GIRL, TRAPPED (Book #8)
GIRL, EXPENDABLE (Book #9)
GIRL, ESCAPED (Book #10)
GIRL, HIS (Book #11)
GIRL, LURED (Book #12)
GIRL, MISSING (Book #13)
GIRL, UNKNOWN (Book #14)

LAURA FROST FBI SUSPENSE THRILLER
ALREADY GONE (Book #1)
ALREADY SEEN (Book #2)
ALREADY TRAPPED (Book #3)
ALREADY MISSING (Book #4)
ALREADY DEAD (Book #5)
ALREADY TAKEN (Book #6)
ALREADY CHOSEN (Book #7)
ALREADY LOST (Book #8)
ALREADY HIS (Book #9)
ALREADY LURED (Book #10)
ALREADY COLD (Book #11)

EUROPEAN VOYAGE COZY MYSTERY SERIES
MURDER (AND BAKLAVA) (Book #1)
DEATH (AND APPLE STRUDEL) (Book #2)
CRIME (AND LAGER) (Book #3)
MISFORTUNE (AND GOUDA) (Book #4)
CALAMITY (AND A DANISH) (Book #5)
MAYHEM (AND HERRING) (Book #6)

ADELE SHARP MYSTERY SERIES

LEFT TO DIE (Book #1)
LEFT TO RUN (Book #2)
LEFT TO HIDE (Book #3)
LEFT TO KILL (Book #4)
LEFT TO MURDER (Book #5)
LEFT TO ENVY (Book #6)
LEFT TO LAPSE (Book #7)
LEFT TO VANISH (Book #8)
LEFT TO HUNT (Book #9)
LEFT TO FEAR (Book #10)
LEFT TO PREY (Book #11)
LEFT TO LURE (Book #12)
LEFT TO CRAVE (Book #13)
LEFT TO LOATHE (Book #14)
LEFT TO HARM (Book #15)
LEFT TO RUIN (Book #16)

THE AU PAIR SERIES
ALMOST GONE (Book#1)
ALMOST LOST (Book #2)
ALMOST DEAD (Book #3)

ZOE PRIME MYSTERY SERIES
FACE OF DEATH (Book#1)
FACE OF MURDER (Book #2)
FACE OF FEAR (Book #3)
FACE OF MADNESS (Book #4)
FACE OF FURY (Book #5)
FACE OF DARKNESS (Book #6)

A JESSIE HUNT PSYCHOLOGICAL SUSPENSE SERIES
THE PERFECT WIFE (Book #1)
THE PERFECT BLOCK (Book #2)
THE PERFECT HOUSE (Book #3)
THE PERFECT SMILE (Book #4)
THE PERFECT LIE (Book #5)
THE PERFECT LOOK (Book #6)
THE PERFECT AFFAIR (Book #7)
THE PERFECT ALIBI (Book #8)
THE PERFECT NEIGHBOR (Book #9)
THE PERFECT DISGUISE (Book #10)

THE PERFECT SECRET (Book #11)
THE PERFECT FAÇADE (Book #12)
THE PERFECT IMPRESSION (Book #13)
THE PERFECT DECEIT (Book #14)
THE PERFECT MISTRESS (Book #15)
THE PERFECT IMAGE (Book #16)
THE PERFECT VEIL (Book #17)
THE PERFECT INDISCRETION (Book #18)
THE PERFECT RUMOR (Book #19)
THE PERFECT COUPLE (Book #20)
THE PERFECT MURDER (Book #21)
THE PERFECT HUSBAND (Book #22)
THE PERFECT SCANDAL (Book #23)
THE PERFECT MASK (Book #24)
THE PERFECT RUSE (Book #25)
THE PERFECT VENEER (Book #26)

CHLOE FINE PSYCHOLOGICAL SUSPENSE SERIES
NEXT DOOR (Book #1)
A NEIGHBOR'S LIE (Book #2)
CUL DE SAC (Book #3)
SILENT NEIGHBOR (Book #4)
HOMECOMING (Book #5)
TINTED WINDOWS (Book #6)

KATE WISE MYSTERY SERIES
IF SHE KNEW (Book #1)
IF SHE SAW (Book #2)
IF SHE RAN (Book #3)
IF SHE HID (Book #4)
IF SHE FLED (Book #5)
IF SHE FEARED (Book #6)
IF SHE HEARD (Book #7)

THE MAKING OF RILEY PAIGE SERIES
WATCHING (Book #1)
WAITING (Book #2)
LURING (Book #3)
TAKING (Book #4)
STALKING (Book #5)
KILLING (Book #6)

PROLOGUE

"Run, Sammy!" Susie screamed, her throat raw and sore. "Run!" She sprinted, clutching her sides. Her lungs felt as if they were on fire, and she struggled to breathe. She had never run so hard or so fast in her life. The dark night spread before them, only the half-moon illuminating their path. The hulking woods were deathly quiet. There was a telltale whistle and then the sound of branches cracking. Her heart pounded in her ears. She was sure she was going to die.

The ATV lights suddenly brightened up the road.

Susie looked behind.

He was gaining on them.

Sammy cried from exhaustion and fell to her knees, but Susie ran back and grabbed her, lifting her up by her elbow. They were twins, but Susie had always been the athletic one, while Sammy preferred to read books. Susie dragged her sister off to the side as the man's voice bellowed through the night:

"Soooooie!" he called out, cackling and laughing. "Squeee! Come on, girls, round 'em up!"

They needed to get off the road. Susie dragged Sammy into the brush, where their feet sank into the swampy mud, making them soaking wet. But they had to get away. Even if there were alligators. Even if there were other animals who could eat them in the night.

It would be better than the deranged man who was pursuing them.

Susie thought back to earlier.

What had started it all?

It had been a normal day. The girls were at their family cottage by themselves for the first time. At twenty, they were old enough now. But part of them were still the same kids they'd always been when they came up here. They had been playing with a little garter snake outside of the cottage as the sun set.

Sammy loved animals, and though Susie didn't share her fascination, she tried her best to care for them. They had found the little brown and green snake, and Sammy had decided to keep it in their room, even as Susie protested.

"C'mon, Susie," Sammy had said, her brown eyes pleading. "Can't you just let me keep my little snake? I'll keep it away from you, I promise."

Susie looked down, her hands on her hips. "That thing is creepy," she had said. "Just throw it back into the wild."

Then a man had crept up to the cottage in an ATV. "How are you girls doing?" he'd asked.

The cottage was remote, not many people around, so seeing a neighbor they'd never seen before was rare.

And that was the first red flag.

From there, the rest of the night became a blur that had led them to this moment. The man had threatened them with a shotgun and told them to run. Now, they were stuck in this deadly game of cat and mouse.

Susie pushed her way through the brush, Sammy right behind her, until they stumbled onto a patch of wet grass.

"What now?" Sammy asked, her eyes wide and wet with tears.

"I don't know," Susie breathed. "I don't know." She hugged her sister and cradled her head in her arms.

"I'm scared, Susie," Sammy said, her voice small and trembling.

"I know, Sam," Susie said as she rubbed Sammy's hair with her palm.

In the distance, they could hear him yelling, hollering: "Soooie!"

"We have to keep moving," Susie said, looking deep into Sammy's eyes. "Come on. You have to run, Sammy. You have to."

The girls ran until they found a tree whose branches hung low, almost touching the ground.

"Keep going," Susie said, but her lungs were burning. When she didn't hear Sammy, she turned around, peering into the dark Florida wetlands.

Sammy wasn't there.

"Sammy!" she cried in a hoarse whisper. "Sammy!"

But there was no answer, no sound of running footsteps, no rustling in the bushes.

"Sammy!" Susie called again. Fear crept into her heart as she paced around, looking everywhere. Where was her sister?

Then, like a beacon of light, Sammy's voice cried out: "I'm here, I'm here! Help, I'm stuck!"

Susie whipped in the direction of the sound, and there was her sister, her leg half-trapped in deep mud. "I can't move!" Sammy shouted, trying to pull herself away.

Susie looked around in the dark, her heart racing. What should I do? What should I do?

Then she made a decision and ran to her sister, sinking into the mud up to her knees. She reached for Sammy as she pulled a clump of weeds from the ground, attempting to clear the way for Sammy to get herself out, but it was no use. She needed to do more. "I'm going to pull you out," Susie said. "But you have to help me."

Sammy nodded, the tears still in her eyes, the fear still in her heart.

"On the count of three," Susie said. "One, two, three."

Sammy screamed out, her hands struggling against the mud. Susie tugged as hard as she could, but Sammy wouldn't break free.

"I can't get loose," Sammy choked. "Please help me, Susie!"

"I'm trying," Susie said, trying to keep her voice level to ease her sister's panic.

Then the ATV lights appeared.

Susie and Sammy looked into them.

And the last thing they saw was the vehicle barreling toward them through the swamp. The voice echoed into the night, piercing their ears.

"Soooie!"

CHAPTER ONE

Agent Nicky Lyons, FBI BAU specialist, sat across from her date in the comfortable booth. It wasn't often that she got to relax like this. Her childhood friend, Matt Haynes, looked shy as he chatted about his life over the past several years they'd been apart. This was their first time seeing each other since they'd graduated high school, but they were both a long way from West Virginia—this was Florida, after all, and a much different environment. But Matt was used to traveling the world.

"So then I went to Thailand, which has the best street food, by the way," Matt told her. Sandy-blond hair brushed over his forehead, and Nicky smiled, nodding, as he talked.

The atmosphere of the restaurant was light, musical, and warm as a ray of the last golden light of day filtered through the window. The musician played the blues on his saxophone and had missed the audience by only an inch.

Nicky had spent so much time lately thinking about her sister, Rosie, and how she'd disappeared so many years ago, when Nicky was sixteen and Rosie was fifteen. Just a couple of days ago, Nicky had decided that she was going to reopen the cold case of Rosie Lyons—officially, although on her own terms. She hadn't talked to her boss about it yet, biding her time for the right moment to get Chief Franco alone.

For now, she was here with Matt, and she had to admit it was nice to relax with a glass of wine and the company of someone she'd known for so long.

Matt hadn't changed much since high school in terms of his personality—he was still a cheery go-getter—but physically, he'd put on a lot of lean muscle and looked more ruggedly handsome than ever before.

Nicky had to admit, she liked the way he'd changed.

"So how long will you be in town?" Nicky asked.

Matt shrugged. "I don't know. I've been on the road for the past year and I'm ready to settle down. I'm thinking about getting a place in South Florida, near my sister, actually."

Nicky raised an eyebrow. "I didn't know Lily moved to South Florida."

Lily was only a year younger than Nicky and Matt, and they'd all grown up next door to each other. Even though Lily hadn't been as close to Nicky as Matt had been, they'd still been good friends.

Matt nodded. "She got married a few years ago to some rich guy and moved here. She has two kids now, a son and a daughter. I know she'd like to see you again."

Nicky stared at Matt. A feeling of dread had come over her, and she was pretty sure she knew why. Lily had been Rosie's best friend, and Nicky hadn't thought about her in a while. She thought of Lily, living a life that maybe Rosie would've had if she hadn't been taken away.

Matt smiled. "I think I'm ready to settle down, really settle down. I mean, I'm already thirty. It'll be nice to have family close by."

Nicky nodded, but she found herself distracted by thoughts of Rosie.

"Anyway, enough about me," Matt said. "Tell me how the FBI thing is going. I feel like I don't know you anymore since I've been away."

Nicky smiled and tried to stay in the moment. "That's because you don't know me. I've changed so much, you wouldn't even recognize me."

Matt raised an eyebrow. "That good, huh?"

"So-so," Nicky said with a shrug. "I focus on finding missing girls, actually."

A silence hung between them. Of course, Matt had been there when Rosie never came home. He had comforted Nicky after Nicky had returned—after all, both Nicky and Rosie had been kidnapped. Nicky was able to escape. Rosie, on the other hand, was never seen again.

But Matt, clearly trying to keep the moment light, just smiled and nodded. "Wow, that's great, Nic. I bet you've saved a lot of lives."

"Some," Nicky said, then she went quiet, unable to stop the images of the girls she couldn't save from flashing through her mind.

Matt reached across the table and put a hand on her arm. "You can't save everyone, Nic."

5

Nicky nodded. She knew that. She knew she couldn't save everyone, but she did everything in her power to try. A lot of her job was saving people… but it wasn't always possible.

Matt smiled, almost apologetically, and withdrew his hand. He took a sip of his beer. "I didn't mean to bring up anything too heavy. Sorry."

Nicky blinked, then nodded. "I know you didn't. You're right, though… I want to save people, and sometimes I can't. It's just part of the job."

Matt didn't say anything, just took another sip of beer.

"Listen, I'm actually glad we're having this conversation," Nicky said. "I think it's time I started looking into Rosie again—I mean, officially."

Matt raised an eyebrow. "You're going to ask your boss about reopening Rosie's case?"

Nicky nodded. "I think I have to, Matt."

Matt smiled. "I'm proud of you, Nic. I think you need to do that."

Nicky smiled, then sat up a little straighter. "Thank you, Matt."

Matt smiled back at her, and they both took a sip of their drinks.

Time flew by as their conversation delved deeper into the good old days. "I remember you used to be such a party animal," Matt teased, and Nicky smiled, brushing it off.

"I wasn't that bad," she said with a laugh.

"Oh, you were bad," Matt said. "You could drink like a fish. But you never ended up passing out at any parties."

"Of course not. That was your job."

They both chuckled. Nicky was enjoying talking to Matt, although it wasn't easy to think about those old days. Still, Nicky had to admit it was good to get it out of her head. Their food arrived, and they tucked into bowls of hearty pasta. Nicky felt herself unwind, her body becoming loose.

Matt had a way of lightening her up, and she needed that—she needed to laugh a little, to feel light.

She felt herself becoming attracted to Matt, and she couldn't deny it. His smile was a little too charming, and she knew he'd been with a lot of women, but she'd always had a soft spot for him.

Yes, she'd really needed this date.

It was a good thing, she told herself, that they had a lot of catching up to do.

Maybe she'd just enjoy herself.

Nicky couldn't remember the last time she'd felt this relaxed. The musician had made his way to the back of the restaurant and was taking a break. The restaurant was mostly empty at this time of night, with no more than a few couples and single people scattered throughout.

She felt good. It was nice to share a meal and a glass of wine with an old friend.

Clearly, judging by the look in his eyes, Matt felt the same way.

In high school, she and Matt had been close. They'd had a group of solid friends whom they'd hung out with every weekend and went on walks with during the sunsets back in West Virginia. Nicky didn't think about those days often—her mind was always preoccupied with work, with thoughts of Rosie. But when she did think of them, they were happy memories for her.

Nicky glanced out the window. The sun had dipped below the horizon, and the stars were emerging over the buildings of Jacksonville.

Nicky's phone rang, and she saw that it was Chief Franco. She excused herself from the table and answered the call.

"What's going on, Chief?" she asked.

"We've got a situation, Nicky," he said. "I need you to come down to the office."

"What's going on?" she asked again, her heart rate starting to increase.

"I'll explain when you get here," he said. "It's about one of the missing women from the list… in fact, the last one on the list. We have some intel that has just made it a top priority. You need to get here."

Nicky's palms grew sweaty. She'd had a couple drinks, having had no idea she'd be going back to work tonight—but that was fine. She could handle it.

"Will do, Chief," she said. "See you shortly."

She glanced across the restaurant at Matt and felt a pang of guilt that she'd have to cut their date short.

But she'd been waiting for this moment for a long time, and now it had finally come.

"I'm sorry, Matt," she said back at the table, sliding her phone into her purse. "I have to go. Work stuff."

Matt looked at her, his eyes dark, and nodded. "Hey, I understand. You're an important person now."

She smiled, feeling bad. "I'll call you tomorrow."

Matt smiled too. "I'll be waiting."

"I'll see you soon, Matt. I'm glad we had this time together."

Matt nodded at her, and she gave him a kiss on the cheek, the same way he'd given her a kiss on the cheek the last time they'd seen each other. She felt warmth in her chest, and she thought again how nice it was to have him there with her.

"I'll see you soon, Nicky," he said.

Nicky smiled again, then left some cash on the table and headed for the door.

"Hold on," Matt called after her, "it was on me!"

Nicky shot him a grin over her shoulder. "You can get the next one."

Then she was outside, into the warm evening. She was trying to play it cool, but the chief's call had her mind on high alert.

If this was enough to get the tenth woman on the list put to number one, then it must be huge.

As she walked, her mind began to race. She thought about the woman and where she might be. She hoped she was still alive. That would make everything easier.

But if she was dead, and there was some sort of proof…

No. She didn't want to think about it.

She had to get to work.

CHAPTER TWO

Nicky paced into the briefing room back at HQ, where Chief Franco was already sitting. Grace Taylor, the young tech on Nicky's team, and Ken Walker, Nicky's partner, were also at the table. It was dark outside, and through the windows, the skyline of Jacksonville was lit up like fireflies. As a BAU agent with the FBI, Nicky specialized in behavioral analysis and catching kidnappers and killers—particularly with a focus on missing girls cases. Chief Eric Franco was her boss, while Nicky was spearheading the team. They'd only worked one case together, but so far, things were going smoothly.

"Agent Lyons, glad you could make it," Franco said, motioning to the table.

Nicky sat down, her heart racing. She needed to know what was going on. Ken wore a grim expression on his face, while Grace looked exhausted, her hair frazzled, like she'd been pulled out of bed. Nicky felt severely underdressed when she realized she was still wearing the jeans and shirt she'd worn on the date with Matt.

"I'm sorry to have to bring you in on this so late," Franco said. "But we've just received some new information that has made this case a top priority."

"What is it?" Nicky asked.

The chief sighed. "You remember the list of ten women we conjured up?"

Nicky nodded. Of course she remembered. That wasn't just a list of names to Nicky—it was a list of people to save, given to her by Senator Amara Gregory of Florida. Nicky and her team were in charge of finding out what happened to those girls. They'd already saved one—there were nine more to go.

"Some of them have been missing for at least three years, making them cold cases," the chief continued. "Others were more recent. You already saved Meghan Salinger, which was stellar work, but the others on that list are still missing."

"Right," Nicky said. "So what's the new information?"

"You might remember that the last two women on the list were twin sisters."

Nicky nodded. "They went missing ten months ago and their case was going nowhere. I remember."

"Yes, London and Paris Knight. Rich girls, transplants from California who'd moved here to get away from the hustle and bustle of LA, I guess," the chief went on. His eyes skated over the team, all eager to hear what the chief had. "Their case was interesting because they both vanished sometime in the night, while they were at a vacation home pretty far out in the bush." Chief pulled a piece of paper out of the file in front of him and slid it down to Nicky. Grace and Ken leaned over the table as well to take a look.

"This is what the kidnapper left behind," Chief said.

It was just a photo of two little tchotchke dolls. They were two inches tall and made of a porcelain or ceramic that looked like it had gone out of style at least a decade ago. The photos were blown up, so the details were crystal clear, but there wasn't much to see in the first place. They were plainly dolls, stylized and colored, really, but the sort of things that wouldn't have been out of place in a little girl's room. Each was wearing a dress with heels on their feet, and each had gold loop earrings. Their hair was long and dark, nearly black, and their eyes seemed to be made of glass.

A chill ran up Nicky's spine. This was creepy. When researching the women on the list, Nicky hadn't gone into the gritty details of every case yet, so this was new to her.

"That gave me the creeps," Grace said, shivering.

Ken nodded in agreement. "Yeah, I'd be happy to never see one of those things again."

Nicky slid the paper back over to Chief. "So what's the new information?"

"Well, as you all know, this case officially went cold; we had no evidence, no leads… and no more victims." The chief sighed. "Until now."

Nicky's stomach bottomed out. She knew what that meant. "There were more victims?"

The chief nodded, face grim. "Twin sisters, twenty years old, just like London and Paris at the time of their disappearances. They were taken near their family cottage, and the killer left behind similar dolls."

"Jesus," Ken said. "When did this happen?"

"It must've been a couple nights ago," Ken said. "When the girls didn't answer their phones, their parents came in looking for them at their cottage, and they were gone. Local police started a search, and then they found... the dolls. One of the officers was familiar with the story."

Nicky leaned back in her chair. She had a lot of questions, but there was a sick, churning feeling in the pit of her stomach and there was only one thing she could think of.

Two sisters, vanishing in the night...

She couldn't help but think of her own story, of what happened with her and Rosie all those years ago. It was different, of course; the man had taken them while the sun was still up, from the suburbs, at gunpoint. Plus, Nicky and Rosie were teenagers, not in their twenties, and they weren't twins either.

But still. The situation was all too familiar, and Nicky wondered if these girls were being taken to a similar place Nicky and Rosie had been taken all those years ago. The lake house... it still haunted Nicky's dreams, and at the same time, it comforted her to think about it.

Sometimes she dreamt of that murky water, flowing above her head, and it brought her to a place of solace.

Only because that was the place where Nicky was last with Rosie. And in some sick, twisted way, that made it a happy place for her.

Nicky cleared her throat and refocused on the moment. This wasn't about her and Rosie—it was about these new victims, and the ones who'd gone missing before.

"So who are the new two?" Nicky asked.

The chief took out another piece of paper and slid it over to Nicky.

"Susie and Sammy Miller," he said.

The photo was of red-haired twins with freckles splattered over their cheeks. They were barely older than twenty, and caught in the moment with smiles on their faces and little squints in their eyes from the flash. Although the girls looked so much alike, one was rounder while the other one had an athletic build.

"Freshly twenty, from a big family, but the girls were at the cottage alone for the first time, according to the family. They're fairly wealthy, not as much as the other two, but still very well off."

Nicky's throat felt tight. She felt for these girls, and for what they must have gone through. She needed to find them and keep them safe—

because if she could solve this case and save them, maybe she could save her own sister, too. She still needed to talk to the chief about reopening Rosie's case, but she needed to do it at the right time. And with a fresh case like this on her lap, she knew she needed to wait a little longer, as much as it hurt to do.

"This case is going to be a priority," Chief Franco said. "We're going to get to the bottom of this, and we're going to keep these girls safe. Lyons, you're the head of this team. Where do you want to start?"

Nicky felt the pressure as Ken and Grace looked at her. Nicky felt like she'd done a good job as leader on the last case, but it was still a lot of responsibility, and she couldn't mess it up. Being twenty-nine and in charge of a team this important was a big feat, but Nicky was determined to prove herself as the strong leader she knew she could be.

She thought over her options and quickly came up with a game plan that would at least cover the first steps of the case.

"Grace," Nicky said, "you can look into the background of the original case, see if you can find any new information. You're welcome to work from home tonight, but I expect you to put in at least a full day tomorrow."

Grace nodded. "You got it, Agent Lyons."

Nicky looked at Ken, whose steely blue eyes were on her, waiting for instruction. "Walker," Nicky said. "You and I should head to the crime scene."

"Right now?" Ken asked, raising a thick eyebrow. "It's after dark."

Nicky nodded. "The sooner we get started, the sooner we can find these girls. Plus, we can assume these girls went missing in the dark, so we'll be able to see the scene as they saw it. I'll contact the local police and get them to let us in."

Ken hesitated, but nodded. "You lead the charge then."

The chief stood up. "Good. Now get out of here, you three. I know you'll all do great things, and I'm proud to have all of you on this team. Go get them."

Nicky smiled, Ken and Grace standing up and giving their goodbyes before following Nicky to the door.

But as Nicky and the others made their way to the elevator, walking through the quiet office, Nicky couldn't shake the nerves from her gut.

She had a strong feeling this case was going to hit a little too close to home.

CHAPTER THREE

An entire area of the swamp was barred off by caution tape, and flashlights illuminated the night. Nicky's feet, adorned with heavy rain boots, sloshed through the mud as she made her way toward the middle of the chaos. Ken was right behind her, his flashlight pointing in all different directions, but all they could see was mud and grass. The air was so humid, Nicky felt like she was swimming.

"Better hope we don't run into any gators," Nicky muttered to Ken.

He shined his light around, looking for any sign of danger. "I don't think that's a problem," he said. "I think the snakes and bugs will be enough."

Nicky laughed, but it hardly helped to lighten the mood. She was on edge, trying to spot anything out of the ordinary. It was hard to see with all the darkness, and nothing stood out to her—but it didn't mean there wasn't something here.

Nicky looked around, shining her light down into the shallow swamplands beneath them. She tried to imagine what the kidnapper had seen; where he must've stood to watch the girls. How did he get them out here, if their cottage was so far away?

She craned her neck, looking for something out of the ordinary. Considering how humid it was, Nicky guessed there could've been rain recently, which could've wiped away any DNA evidence.

Finally, they reached where the other officers were: the scene of the crime, where the two girls had gone missing, and the dolls had been left in their place.

It was a clearing of grass and mud, at least twenty feet long. To the side, five officers were hard at work, carefully sifting through the grass.

"Agent Lyons, Agent Walker," one of the officers said, walking up to them. "I'm Sheriff Winston. I was told you were coming. Good to meet you." The sheriff was a heavyset man who was sweating in the humidity.

"You too," Nicky said. "We heard the news and had to come out here. What are we looking at?"

He took a deep breath. "It stormed the day after the girls were reported missing, so any DNA is long gone. Not a trace," he said, shaking his head. He looked at the two agents.

"Did you find the dolls?" Nicky asked.

He nodded. "They were nearly obscured by the mud and rain, but yeah. We had the park rangers take them for safekeeping. We bagged them and will send them to you. I gotta say, though, I'm shocked we even found them. We didn't find anything else, but as you can see, we're still here looking."

Nicky and Ken made their way to the back of the clearing, where the police had set up a portable light. Two officers were hard at work there, sifting through the mud with a scarred shovel and a fine-tooth comb.

Nicky looked down at the mud, but all she could see were insects and leaves that had been blown into it. She knew there was absolutely nothing here, or the officers wouldn't be working so hard.

"What have you found so far?" Nicky asked.

"Nothing," Sheriff Winston said. "But we're not giving up. We're going to keep looking until we find something."

Nicky, Ken, and the sheriff walked over to the officers, who looked like they were starting to lose hope that they'd find anything.

"It's so much mud," one of them said. "We've been sifting through this all day and we haven't found anything."

Nicky observed the scene. It was definitely muddy, and anyone walking around here without boots was likely to get stuck. There was a circle marked off by caution tape in the mud.

"Sheriff," Nicky called out, "was this where the dolls were found?"

"That's the spot," the sheriff said.

Nicky looked around, observing. Any footprints would have been washed away. But as she flashed her light into the grass around the clearing, something stood out to her. It looked as though there was a parting in the grass, coming from one direction. Two partings, in fact, evenly apart. It could have just been a natural formation, but something about it seemed man-made.

Nicky took out her phone and snapped a photo with the flash on, just in case. She'd been in this field for long enough to know that when something stood out in her gut, it was better to pay attention to it, even if it ended up not meaning anything.

"Sheriff, what's the next town over?" Nicky asked.

He looked at her quizzically. "Nowhere," he said. "There is no town there, Agent Lyons. It's all swamp. There's just the cottages, but they're so far out. There's a convenience store nearby, but no actual town."

Nicky stared at him. "So it's just swamp, everywhere?"

"Pretty much," he said. "What are you thinking?"

She sighed. "I don't know," she said, looking around. "I've been thinking about what happened to the girls. I'm trying to put myself in the kidnapper's shoes. I'll be honest, the one thing I'm really not sure of is how he got them out here so far."

"The swamp, you mean," Sheriff Winston said. "It's impossible for him to have walked through here with the girls."

Nicky nodded. "Exactly," she said, looking around, thinking.

Just then, Ken appeared beside Nicky. "Lyons, one of the officers said some kid might have heard something."

Nicky frowned and looked at the sheriff. "Is that true?"

"My guys interviewed a few people from the surrounding cottages, but I don't have the full report yet," the sheriff said. "You can find the girls' family at their cottage too, although they weren't there at the time the girls went missing."

Nicky nodded. "Please send me the addresses."

"Will do."

With that, Nicky turned to Ken. "Let's get out of here," she said, and Ken followed. Both of them couldn't be happier to leave this swampland behind and get back on solid ground.

But Nicky was nervous about what she'd find out from the locals. In an area as remote as this, it seemed unlikely there would be many witnesses.

That was probably how this guy was able to get away with this.

Once more, Nicky was reminded of her and Rosie. But she buried it down. This was about Susie and Sammy. And she was going to find out what happened to them.

***

Nicky knocked on the door of the cottage Susie and Sammy were staying in, where they would apparently find the twins' parents. It was a cute little cottage, right up in the mountains, with a rock creek running in front of the house.

The door opened, and a woman stood in the doorway. At first, Nicky thought she was looking at a ghost. The woman looked exactly like Susie, except she was older. Freckles on her pale skin, beautiful carrot hair...

"Mrs. Miller?" Nicky asked. "I'm Agent Nicky Lyons with the FBI, and this is my partner, Agent Walker. I'm sorry for your loss. May we come in?"

The woman nodded. She opened the door wider and allowed Nicky and Ken to step into the quaint cottage. The two looked around. The cottage was nice and cozy, with a stone fireplace and a TV. They could see bearskin rugs on the floor and dried herbs hanging from the ceiling.

"You're Susie and Sammy's mother?" Nicky asked.

Mrs. Miller nodded. "Yes, I am. My husband is out talking to the police again, but he should be home soon. Would you like to come in and sit down?"

"Sure," Nicky said. She and Ken sat down on the sofa, and Mrs. Miller sat across from them in the rocking chair.

"I'm so sorry for your loss," Nicky said. "I know that you must be grieving for Susie and Sammy."

"Yes," she said. "I can't believe they're gone. I'm not ready to accept that."

Nicky looked at her sympathetically. She could tell Mrs. Miller was still reeling from the news. She looked as though she had been crying.

"We're doing everything we can to find them," Nicky said. "Can you tell us anything about Susie and Sammy's visit here? Why did they come up alone?"

"They... said they were old enough," Mrs. Miller said. "They wanted the freedom to have fun, but they promised there was no drinking or anything like that. I think the girls just wanted to spend some time here, bonding."

"Right," Nicky said. "And they didn't have any boyfriends? Any guys they might have brought up here?"

"I really don't think so," Mrs. Miller said. "They were both single."

"Any ex-boyfriends who might try to contact them now?"

"Once in a while, there was a guy," Mrs. Miller said. "But for the most part, the girls kept to themselves. I think they were too busy with school to worry about that."

"Were they close with each other?" Nicky asked. "I heard they were twins, so they probably spent a lot of time together."

"Oh, yes," Mrs. Miller said. "They were always together. They were both very close to their dad and me."

"Were there... any problems?" Nicky asked. She hated doing this, but it was her job to go through all the possibilities.

Thankfully, Ken picked up the line of thought so Nicky didn't have to: "Any reason why they might want to disappear from home?" he asked.

Mrs. Miller looked offended. "No. My girls would never run away, if that's what you're implying."

Nicky nodded. "We do apologize. We're required to ask these questions. From our position, it seems fairly obvious that they were taken against their will."

"I know. I understand," Mrs. Miller said.

"Do you think any of your neighbors might have seen anything?" Ken asked. "Anyone who might be suspicious?"

"I really don't know," she said. "I mean, everyone around here is pretty friendly. But there's not a lot of people up here, and I don't know if anyone saw anything."

"We're going to try to find out, I promise," Nicky said. "We heard someone may have seen something, so we're going to talk to them next."

Mrs. Miller nodded. "Thank you." There was a long pause before she said, "A lot of girls are taken against their will. I don't want to assume the worst, but human trafficking is a big problem, and one of my biggest fears as a mother. I'm sure you're aware of that."

"Yes," Nicky said. "But as of right now, we have no reason to believe your daughters are being trafficked." Exchanging a look with Ken, Nicky took out a card from her pocket. She slid it across the kitchen table to Mrs. Miller. "Please contact me personally if anything comes up."

"Thank you," Mrs. Miller said. "I'm very grateful for your help."

Nicky and Ken stood up to leave. "Thank you for your time," Nicky said. "I have to ask you, though—do you have any idea why someone would want to hurt your girls?"

Mrs. Miller looked down. "I wish I did," she said. "The thought of someone hurting my babies is making me sick."

"We'll do everything we can to bring them home," Nicky said. "I promise." She and Ken said their goodbyes and left. This was bad, Nicky knew that much. It wasn't looking good for the girls.

They left the cottage, stepping into the warm night. They walked down a grassy path toward the little copse of trees where more cottages were.

They were on their way to the next cottage, which was about a hundred yards away, when Nicky looked up to see there was a light on in the window up ahead. In that window, she saw a child, a little boy, peeking through.

"What'd that officer say about someone hearing something?" Nicky asked.

"He didn't say much, just that it was a kid. Said we should go talk to him ourselves."

They picked up the pace. They went up the incline and then arrived at the next cottage. Ken knocked on the door. They waited until the door opened.

"Hello?" the woman in the doorway said. It was a young mother, no older than thirty.

"Hi," Nicky said, "I'm Agent Lyons, and this is Agent Walker. We're with the FBI. We're told someone here may have heard something the other night, when Susie and Sammy Miller went missing."

The young mother sheepishly poked her head out, then called into the house, "Jacob, come here, sweetie!"

A boy appeared next to her in the doorway. He was around eight, with short black hair and deep blue eyes. He was wearing khaki shorts and a white T-shirt. He was looking at the agents warily, like they were going to attack him.

"Hey, bud," Nicky said kindly. "We're with the FBI, and we were wondering if you could tell us what you told those other officers. Did you see anything strange around here the other day?"

"I didn't see anything," the boy said defensively, kicking at the floor. "I... heard something."

The mother looked at them apologetically. "I'm sorry, Agents, I'm not so sure my son really heard what he says he did. He has a very vivid imagination."

"Let's hear him out," Ken cut in. The mother nodded and backed off.

Nicky knelt down so she was at eye level with Jacob, so he could feel safer, like he could trust her. "Can you tell us what you heard, Jacob?"

"I was playing outside," Jacob began, "and I heard something growling. It sounded really close, so I came inside to tell my mom."

"What did it sound like?" Nicky asked gently.

"It sounded like a… a monster," Jacob said, his eyes wide. "I've never heard anything like it before. It was like a really big, scary bear."

"Did you see anything?" Ken cut in.

"No, I didn't see anything," Jacob said. "But it sounded really close, like it was right outside our house."

The mother put a hand on her son's shoulder. Tears welled up in the young boy's eyes, and his mother wrapped her arms around him protectively. "I'm sorry, Agents," she said quietly. "My son has been having nightmares ever since it happened."

Nicky stood up slowly, her mind racing with possibilities. If what Jacob had heard was true, then could there be a large animal in the area? No, it wouldn't make sense. The dolls were left at the crime scene, and if an animal had attacked Susie and Sammy, then there would have been carnage left behind.

Unless the animal was what got them out into the wilderness?

The only issue with that was that there were no bears in the area. Nicky thanked the family for their time, but she had no idea what to think of this information—or if it was helpful at all.

CHAPTER FOUR

His feet creaked against the floor as he made his way down the hallway, his stomach roiling with joy. Ten months, and he'd finally made another catch. Wasn't so easy, pulling something like this off, and he'd tried many times over the years with no luck.

But this time was different.

He was finally one step closer to getting the family together. It'd all be worth the wait.

For a better part of thirty years, he'd been doing this. Never been caught. The dolls were a newer touch; it'd make those cops chase their tails, and the thought brought a smile to his face. They could go ahead and chase each other around like pigs in the mud for all he cared.

He had his new girls—two beautiful twins—and that was all that mattered.

As he made his way through the house, he could hear pounding on the walls. One of the twins, the skinnier one, had some fight in her. Feisty. He liked that.

She'd be fun to play with.

The pounding grew louder, and he could hear the faint squeaking of nails on the floor, coming from the room on his left. He'd need to fix that, but not yet. It'd be best if the house took care of that itself.

The other twin was much quieter. She wouldn't be much fun, but she had to be there. She was a part of the family. It wasn't right otherwise.

The pounding grew louder, and he could hear his lovely little doll screaming now. It was still muffled, but not for long. He knew what had to be done.

The pounding grew louder still as he drew closer to their room, until he was right beside the door. The girls must have heard his feet creak against the floor, because everything went dead silent.

"*Bare rolig, lille skat,*" he spoke through the door. "*Det bliver fint.*"

They wouldn't understand his Danish, but they didn't need to. "*Når vi bliver gift, vil alt være perfekt,*" he murmured.

The banging started back up. He flinched away from the shifting door, then looked at it with a smile.

"Let us out of here!" The skinnier twin banged roughly on the door and screamed. "You freak, let us go!"

"*Nå, nu, lille gris…*" Now, now, little pig…

"Let us out!" The other twin started banging on the door as well. She was more polite than her sister, and her voice was sweeter. It was going to be hard to choose between them. Both had such promise. Both were so supple and beautiful, and just the perfect age; not too young, not too old.

"Not so fast, *min lille gris.*" He laughed, patting the doorknob.

The pounding grew louder still and his smile widened.

"*Alt vil fungere lige som jeg ønsker det.*"

Everything will work out just as I want it to.

The pounding continued, but the skinnier twin had fallen silent. He wondered what she was thinking. They were frightened now, but they would come around. They always did.

He tilted his head to one side, listening to the pounding and the creaking on the door. The walls were shaking a little now, and he could hear another sound.

The skinnier twin started crying.

His face fell. It was hard enough trying to choose one of the twins, and now they were both going to be upset. He didn't want to hurt them like this. He'd be sure to take away their sadness.

He knocked on the door. "I will take care of you, *lille skat.* I promise."

Silence.

"Do not worry." His hand drifted to the doorknob. "Everything will be better soon. You will see. The walls will swallow you and I will be a good husband and I will make you happy. You will see."

Silence.

"*Vi bliver gift.*"

We will be married.

"Shhh…" He waved a hand at the door. "*Så slemt bliver det ikke. Bare rolig,*" he whispered. That's not so bad. Just relax.

The pounding stopped.

"*Ikke vær bange.*" Don't be afraid.

"*Ikke bange; jeg skal nok passe godt på jer.*" Don't be afraid; I'll take care of you.

21

CHAPTER FIVE

Morning sunlight filtered through the curtains as Nicky stretched, sitting at the table at the motel. Nicky was never a fan of staying at motels, but at least at this one, she and Ken had been able to get separate beds. It was still the same room, but after they'd been in such close quarters during their last case, it wasn't a big deal. Besides, it was slim pickings in such a rural part of South Florida, and they'd found this lone place off the highway, forty minutes from the cottages Susie and Sammy were staying at.

The door opened, and Ken walked in holding two paper cups of coffee. "I think this might be yesterday's," he said.

Nicky accepted it and gave it a sniff. It definitely smelled stale. But it would do. As far as motels went, this was probably the worst one Nicky had ever stayed at—the mattress had been beyond stiff, the blanket itchy, and Nicky had stared at the peeling ceiling all night long, thinking of Rosie. But still. She'd survived the night, and now that the sun was up, they could get this investigation going for real.

"Better than nothing," she said. "I just hope I don't bring home bed bugs from this place."

"A full fumigation would be bad for business," Ken agreed, sitting across from her.

Nicky had her laptop in front of her. She took a sip of the bitter, burnt-tasting coffee. Good enough.

"So," Ken said, "where do we start today?"

Nicky turned her screen so Ken could see, and they shuffled their chairs closer to each other at the small round table. "I'm going over the notes Grace sent me about the other two missing girls, London and Paris Knight."

"Anything useful?" Ken asked.

"Well, they were the same age as Susie and Sammy—twenty. Of course, that was ten months ago, so they could be twenty-one now." If they're even alive, Nicky thought grimly. She continued, "They were taken on the other side of Florida, though, so pretty far from here. Still, the MO is the exact same."

Nicky brought up a photo of the girls. London Knight was tall and slender, with bleach-blonde hair. Paris Knight was shorter, stouter, with black hair.

"As you can see, their hair colors are completely different from Susie and Sammy," Nicky said. "But one thing I did note was that each twin has a similar build to one of the twins in the other set. One is taller and more visibly athletic, while the other is a bit shorter and rounder."

Ken leaned back in the chair and ran a hand over his clean-shaven jawline. "I wonder if it means anything."

"The body types, you mean?" Nicky said. "I was thinking that. I mean, our guy's ramping up his activity. It's like he's made a decision to get back into the game."

"So?" Ken frowned.

"So…" Nicky ran her fingers through her long, straight brown hair. "Maybe he likes the variety of having two girls with different body types."

"Why not just kidnap two friends, then?" Ken asked.

Nicky nodded. "A good point. I'm not sure what all of this means. Susie and Sammy are nearly identical except for their builds. At this point, it's hard to say what this guy is after."

"Whatever it is, we need to find a connection that links all of these girls," Ken said. "Grace's already found that they lived in different parts of Florida, right?"

"Yeah. Grace is checking with their family, but she's not getting a lot of help." Nicky sighed. She didn't tell Ken that Grace had also mentioned that they might run into problems with the Knight family. The Knights had apparently hired a PI and refused to talk to the police because they found them incompetent and untrustworthy. Nicky understood that. But according to Grace, the PI never found any clues either.

Ken stood up from his chair and stretched. "I'm going to go get something to eat," he said. "Want anything?"

"A huge stack of pancakes, a pound of bacon, and some maple syrup."

"Okay." Ken grinned. "I can swing that."

"Do I even want to know what you're having?" Nicky asked him.

"Just something light," Ken said. "I have a feeling we're going to be running a lot today."

Nicky nodded. "Well, if we don't get any answers, at least you'll be in good shape. I need some fuel to keep me going."

"That's true," Ken said. "I'll be back in a bit."

"Thanks," Nicky said as he left. She opened up a new document and started typing up profiles of the missing girls as well as what they'd found so far on Susie and Sammy.

Nothing yet stood out, but Nicky knew that it was necessary to keep going over details, over and over, even when it felt like they weren't going to find anything. Nicky took a sip of her now-cold coffee, frowning. What was the connection between these two sets of twins, other than the fact that they were twins?

Well, they were young, and young people loved social media. Nicky decided to turn her attention there, see what she could dig up about all of them—their friendships, their dating histories…

She started with Susie and Sammy's Facebook accounts. They were public, of course, and their photos and posts had been shared all over the internet. Nicky clicked around, looking for anything that might be useful.

From what she could see, the girls were pretty typical young women, and not just in the fact that they were identical twins. They'd shared photos of their friends. They'd taken selfies with their phones and posted them on Instagram. They were college students, so they'd posted a lot of memes and quotes about studying and partying and the like.

It was the usual stuff, but Nicky saved it all anyway. She had to start somewhere, and the internet was a good place to look. She moved on to Paris and London, who seemed much more outgoing than their Florida counterparts. London and Paris were clearly partiers. Their social media was full of opulent-looking club photos and pictures taken on the beach.

All of these young women were gorgeous, and surely hot ticket items for the boys in their towns. When something bad happened to a woman, it was typical to first look at her boyfriend or husband. But according to Susie and Sammy's parents, they were single. And according to London and Paris's social media…

They were also single.

Maybe there was a connection there.

She glanced around the room, still taking in the dingy, rundown state of the motel.

The motel room itself was furnished with two single beds, a dresser, and a small table with two chairs. But the carpet and the walls were so old that the room looked like it was melting into the floorboards.

The window was open, letting in the sounds of traffic from the road. Nicky heard a horn blow, a dog bark, and a child cry. She closed the door to block out some of the noise, and then turned her attention back to the laptop. The only people out here were tourists on vacation, or the odd person who lived here and ran the businesses. It really was a lonely place, and an easy place to go missing in.

Nicky wasn't sure if it was a connection that the girls were all single, but something in her told her to look into it, just a little deeper. In the FBI database, she opened up some old case files from the area.

She looked for missing person reports from the past several years, with young women who were single, recently broken up with a boyfriend, or who had just gotten divorced. There hadn't been a lot of violent crime in this area.

Nicky could spend hours combing through cases and it could land her nowhere. She was looking for something specific—anything that mentioned girls being "single." So, she decided to search the files for that specific word. She found some witnesses testimonies...

And one of them came from a woman, about ten years ago, about a man who'd been going around the area and asking young women if they were "single."

Nicky's heart rate picked up. It could be nothing—or it could be everything. A creep with a fascination with young, single girls, in the same area? It was worth looking into.

Apparently, the FBI had found this guy worth looking into too, but it never went anywhere. He wasn't charged with anything.

Moving as rapidly as she could, Nicky dug deeper into the file.

That guy may not have been charged, but he did move.

He moved to a town only an hour away from where Susie and Sammy went missing.

Nicky's heart was beating fast as she read over all of the information. This man...he had a history of asking women if they were single.

But was he the one who'd been picking them up?

Nicky glanced over to the motel room door and then closed the laptop. She pulled out her cell phone, pressed a few buttons, and then waited. Ken picked up after the second ring.

"Lyons, I'm still waiting—"

"Forget the breakfast, Walker," Nicky said. "We have a lead."

CHAPTER SIX

Nicky's car was taking a beating from all these backcountry roads, and she found herself missing the rental—only because it wasn't her baby who'd been getting all banged up back in South Florida. But the cottages were only an hour drive from Jacksonville, and so she'd taken on the task of driving here. But now that she and Ken were on their way to the suspect's house, Nicky felt bad for what she was doing to her car all the way out here.

"These roads are relentless," Nicky said as she dodged another pothole. The early morning sun glared in her eyes, bouncing off the black paint of her car.

Ken was quiet as she drove. He had his laptop out and was reviewing

"Listen to this," he said. "It's a transcript from our suspect, an interview an agent did with him."

"Interview?"

"Yeah, they had him in for questioning then let him go," Ken said. "The agent talked to him but got nowhere. There was nothing to charge him with, and the guy was just too weird."

"Interesting," Nicky said. "Do you have the recording?"

"Right here." Ken pressed play, and they both listened intently to the recording.

"This is Special Agent Drake Jones of the FBI, Florida division, interviewing Suspect A, Yancy Rosen."

Nicky exchanged a look with Ken as the recording played, filling the car. Nicky didn't know this Drake Jones guy, but this recording was from over a decade ago.

"What were you doing near those women, Yancy?" Drake asked on the recording.

"What... what women?" Yancy asked. His voice was snakelike and small. It sent a chill up Nicky's spine.

"You were seen near the university," Drake said. *"Near the apartments. You were asking young women if they were single. You're not married, are you, Yancy? You're not seeing anyone?"*

"No, no... I don't want to date anyone," Yancy said. "I'm too busy for that."

"So you were looking for young women who were single?" Drake asked.

"I was just... just getting the lay of the land," Yancy said. "You know, looking for places where I could have lunch. Maybe have a sandwich."

Drake's voice grew louder and sharper on the recording, and he said, "So you're telling me that you were looking for a place to eat lunch and you started talking to all these young women, asking them if they're single, making them uncomfortable?"

"They're very beautiful," Yancy said in a meek voice. "What's wrong with admiring perfection?"

"I don't see your wife in here," Drake replied. "You're not married, right? So you must be looking for someone single."

"I... I never did anything. I just looked at some beautiful girls. It's not a crime to look."

"And here's the thing, Yancy," Drake said. "This isn't a crime yet. But if you keep harassing these girls, it will be. I'm giving you a warning. Stop doing this, or you have to deal with me."

"No... no... no..." Yancy said, barely audible on the recording.

Nicky glanced over at Ken. She saw his jaw tensing, and she wondered if he was getting as upset as she was by this recording.

"You are not allowed to have any contact with women in your state," Drake said on the recording. "You are not allowed to meet them, to talk to them. You can't just go up to women and accost them on the street, okay? Do you understand?"

"Yes, sir," Yancy said meekly.

The recording ended, and it was silent in the car. Nicky rounded a corner, and the car swerved a little.

"I don't like this guy," Ken said. "Smarmy."

"I agree," Nicky said. "He's slimy. He wants girls and he wants them to be single. And he's persistent, by the sounds of it. It could be a coincidence, but this guy living so close to where the twins went missing..."

"It's worth the trip," Ken said. "I agree."

"But where the hell is this GPS taking us?" Nicky asked, glancing at her dashboard. They were going deeper into the brush, and by the looks of it, if they kept on this road, they'd reach a lake soon.

Apparently, Yancy lived on the shore of it, but the road they had to take to get there was almost overgrown with weeds. Not many tire tracks had gone through here recently.

"I don't know," Ken said. "But the directions say this is the right way."

They drove on in silence. The sun beat down on them aggressively, bouncing off the black car and the windshield. Nicky squinted, trying to keep her eyes on the road. Then, suddenly—she felt her car slide to the side.

"Oh, shit!" She slammed on the brakes and felt the car spin out and then come crashing to a halt, the car's bumper buried in a thicket of brush.

"What the hell was that?" Ken asked.

"I lost control of the damn thing," Nicky said. Thankfully, when she tried to back away from the brush, the wheels caught traction, and she was able to slowly maneuver back. "These roads aren't built for sedans," Nicky noted. "To travel out here, you'd need something that can handle it, like a Jeep or an ATV." She kept driving, but kept it nice and slow.

"Well, don't kill us," Ken said, visibly frazzled.

Nicky could feel the mud slicking beneath her wheels, but they were too far out now to go back. She had to push on, and according to the GPS, they were close to the lake.

She saw it soon enough—a massive lake that seemed to engulf the small cabin that stood on the shore. It was one floor, and it was surrounded by trees and overgrown brush. Several low-hanging trees spread leaves around their branches and brushed the ground.

"That's gotta be the place," Ken said.

"Let's do it," Nicky said. She slowed to a crawl and then stopped, parking on the side of the road. She and Ken both pulled out their guns and strapped them to their sides. Ken had his gun in his holster while Nicky had hers in her waistband in the small of her back. She had her FBI badge in another pocket.

"Ready?" Ken asked.

"Ready," Nicky said.

They stepped out of the car. Nicky braced herself against the heat and the blasting sun. It wasn't even ten in the morning yet, and it felt like a hundred degrees.

As they crept up to the house, Nicky saw that there was a dock on the other side of the house down by the lake. And moored to it was a speedboat.

And down by the dock, gathering some bait, was Yancy Rosen. Nicky recognized him from his file.

Yancy Rosen was a thin man, with tiny shoulders and a sunken-in chest. He had dark hair that was greased back from his forehead and small, beady eyes. He was wearing a pair of shorts and a sleeveless shirt, showing off badly tattooed arms, and he had a fishing pole in one hand.

Then he spotted them.

Without hesitation, he dropped his bait and pole and jumped into the speedboat moored at the dock.

"Hey!" Nicky shouted. She and Ken both took off running toward the dock, but Yancy was already inside the boat.

The engine roared as Yancy attempted to start it. Nicky pulled ahead of Ken and raced along the dock, her feet pounding against the wood as if it were a sprint track. Yancy got it started. The boat pulled out of the dock.

Yancy didn't see Nicky in time.

Nicky jumped.

She landed hard on the boat, catching herself on her hands and looking up at the staggering Yancy behind the wheel.

"What the hell?!" he shouted. "Get off my boat!"

He tried to put it into gear, but Nicky scrambled to her feet and grabbed the wheel.

"No, you're coming with me," Nicky said, her voice edged with anger. "We're with the FBI. Yancy Rosen, you need to—"

"Get off my boat! It's mine!" Yancy shouted, wrestling for control of the wheel.

Nicky grabbed his arms and wrestled him back. Yancy shoved her, but she held tight. He then threw a leg up and kicked her in the gut, and Nicky flew backwards. Her back banged against the side of the boat, knocking the wind from her lungs.

The wind whipped Nicky's hair around. She hadn't realized the boat was going so fast. It was speeding into the water at an alarming rate, and Ken was still on the dock, his arms raised.

It was up to Nicky to stop Yancy—because he was clearly guilty of something. She could add violence toward an FBI agent to that list.

The boat picked up speed as Nicky struggled to her feet. Her ribs hurt—Yancy had kicked her hard. But she was determined.

Yancy drove the boat straight toward the middle of the lake. A sinking feeling grew in the pit of her stomach. She sprinted forward and grabbed ahold of the wheel, but Yancy shoved her away.

She grabbed at his arm, but he shoved her aside again. This time, she was ready.

With a quick movement, she grabbed his arm and twisted it behind his back. Yancy yelped in pain as Nicky forced him to the ground.

"I'm not going to tell you again," she said through gritted teeth. "Stop the boat."

"Screw you!" Yancy shouted. He was thrashing, trying to throw her off. With one hard thrust, Yancy shot up, sending Nicky flying backwards. At that moment, she wished she were just a bit heavier. Son of a bitch!

"You're not stopping me!" Yancy shouted. "I'll kill you, bitch!"

"I'm not going to warn you again," Nicky said. She stormed up to him and grabbed his arm, clutching his wrist. "Stop the boat or I'll break your arm."

Yancy snarled in anger. He jerked his arm free and shoved her. Nicky stumbled back, but she kept her footing. Yancy leaned over to the side of the boat, where there was a collection of nets. A heavy metal net toppled over, landing over Nicky and triggering a wave of pain. "Leave me alone!" Yancy yelled.

Nicky struggled to get out from underneath the net. The boat was speeding toward the center of the lake, and Ken was still on the dock. He was too far away to help her.

Nicky was done playing around. She pulled out a pocket knife, one she always kept on her in case of emergencies, and shredded through the net as Yancy was back behind the wheel. It looked like he was going to crash them into the shore on the other side. Nicky had to act fast. She quickly wrapped her arms around Yancy's waist and took him to the ground. She applied a choke hold and squeezed tightly until he stopped struggling. Then she pulled out her handcuffs and secured his hands behind his back.

"You're under arrest, Yancy Rosen," she said as she stood up. "You have the right to remain silent. Anything you say can and will be used against you in a court of law. You have the right to an attorney. If you cannot afford an attorney, one will be provided for you. Do you understand these rights?"

"Let me go! I'm innocent!" He struggled like a worm on the floor of the boat.

Nicky left him there to writhe as she dove toward the wheel and took control of the boat, steering it back to the docks, where Ken was waiting. She looked back at Yancy, who'd given up and had curled into a lump on the floor.

Now, all she had to do was take him in.

CHAPTER SEVEN

The drive out of Yancy's area with him handcuffed in the back had been tense, and Nicky was damn grateful to be out of her car and in an interrogation room at the local state police station. It'd taken far too long to travel, and hours of the day had already been wasted—it was lunch now, and Nicky realized that she and Ken still hadn't eaten. Beside her in the interrogation room, Ken looked tired, while Nicky herself was feeling weak.

But it didn't matter. They needed to save face. And Yancy was right in front of them, shivering like a wet dog in the chair.

"Okay, Yancy," Nicky said, "explain to me why you ran from us."

Yancy was a skinny man, with a sickly pale complexion. He looked up at them meekly. Compared to how he'd acted on the boat, Yancy had completely changed character—he'd been dead quiet since they apprehended him, and even now, his voice was so small. "I wasn't running from you," he peeped.

"You were speeding away from us," Ken said. "It looked like you were trying to get away."

"I… was trying to get away from you," Yancy said. "I thought you were here to kill me…"

Ken was silent. Nicky frowned. "We were trying to bring you in for questioning," she said with a sigh. "That's all. You didn't have to run."

"Please let me go," Yancy said. "I haven't done anything wrong."

"What about the fact that you attacked a federal agent?" Ken said. He leaned forward, pressing his hands onto the table. "Your little spectacle on the boat wasn't exactly sudden, Yancy, so let's cut the innocent act."

Nicky nodded in agreement. She wasn't sure she was buying Yancy's meager act, either.

"She was on my boat!" Yancy said. "I thought…" His eyes shifted away from them. "I didn't know who she was. I was scared."

"What were you scared of?" Nicky asked. "Did you think we were coming to arrest you for something?"

33

"I was scared... of you guys." Yancy looked up at them, his eyes wide. "I'm all alone out there, you know. I don't see many people. I didn't know if you were going to hurt me."

Nicky wasn't buying it. Yancy Rosen had some secrets, and she was going to figure out what they were.

"So what do you do for a living, Yancy?" Ken asked. Nicky watched Yancy closely. He was shaking slightly, and she could tell that he was nervous.

"I, well, I help out at the farm... it's not far from where I live, so I can take the tractor out no problem..." He fidgeted with his hands, looking down. "I'm just a simple guy trying to live life."

Nicky had a feeling that it wasn't as simple as he was making it sound. She cleared her throat. "What are you growing on this farm, Yancy?" she asked.

He looked up at her nervously. "Just crops," he said. "I'm a farmer's assistant, more like."

Nicky arched an eyebrow. "You're a farmer who has a record for burglary and stalking women?" she asked. "That doesn't seem like the work of a farmer."

Yancy's eyes flickered between her and Ken. "I, um... what women?"

Nicky and Ken exchanged a look. It was time to stop "getting to know" the perp and get down to business.

"This isn't the first time the FBI has talked to you, is it, Yancy?" Nicky asked, fully knowing the answer. "There was another time. What was it... ten years ago?"

Yancy blanched. He began fidgeting, and he scratched at his neck with his hands, which were now handcuffed in front of him rather than behind his back. His eyes going everywhere.

"You remember, don't you, Yancy?" Nicky asked. "You were caught harassing women, asking them if they were single—"

"I never hurt anyone!" Yancy suddenly shouted. "I was never violent! I just talked to them, asked them if they were single... It wasn't my fault that they got the wrong idea!"

Nicky raised an eyebrow. It was like a switch had been flipped. Yancy had gone from quiet and meek to downright surly, his voice filled with venom. "What the hell is your problem?" Yancy demanded. "I never hurt anyone! It was all harmless fun, nothing more!"

Nicky kept quiet, letting Yancy let it all out until he deflated in the chair.

"I didn't... I wasn't..."

Nicky drew a breath. This guy was clearly unhinged. She was about to press him more, to see what else he would let out in his emotional outburst.

But he spoke first.

"And the single thing, that was just..."

She shot Ken a frown, then leaned forward, listening. "It was what?"

"It was just... there was this guy I knew in my old town... I met him at a bar, you know... he had a thing for twins, I remember that, and he said he was always able to get them to talk to him if he asked if they were single. He liked the single ones."

Twins? Nicky thought. She hadn't even brought up the missing twins yet, and here Yancy was, mentioning twins...

Either he knew about the missing girls and he took them, or he was telling the truth about this odd "friend."

Ken folded his arms. "So that's what you were doing? You were trying to impersonate your friend?"

"Yeah..." Yancy nodded. "I guess... I guess that's what it was."

"You guess?" Nicky asked. She frowned. She wasn't sure she was buying this. "And who is this 'friend'?"

Yancy stared at the tabletop in silence.

Nicky leaned forward. "Are you afraid of him?" she asked. "Is that why you won't tell us who he is?"

Yancy looked up at her, his eyes wide. "I'm not afraid of him!" he snapped. "There's nothing to be afraid of!"

"So go ahead, tell us who he is," Ken said.

Yancy laughed. "That's the thing." He shook his head. "I don't even know who he is... I just met him at a bar. He didn't give me his name."

"And when was this?" Nicky asked.

"Not that long ago. It was before I moved. Two years?"

"If we don't have a name," Nicky said, "how can we know you're even telling us about a real person?"

"He was real!" Yancy exclaimed. "Oh, I—I remember one thing. He had a friend with him. Another man. And they said something about a woman... a woman named Rosie?"

Nicky's heart jerked in her chest.

"What did you just say?" she uttered.

Rosie.

Her sister.

It couldn't be…

Nicky's head spun. She felt the walls of the room closing in around her. The oxygen was sucked out of the air, leaching into some dark corner of the room. Nicky's stomach lurched as her eyes started to water.

"Agent Lyons?"

Nicky turned.

Ken was staring at her, his brow furrowed, his lips pursed. He didn't say anything, and he didn't have to—she could see the worry in his eyes.

She had to get out—now.

Trying to save face—to keep it professional in front of their suspect—Nicky stood up and excused herself. She bolted across the room and out the door, pushing past the officer sitting at the desk and out into the parking lot. Hyperventilating.

CHAPTER EIGHT

His rocking chair creaked as he rocked back and forth, sitting on the porch. Same as always, he was testing the strength of his family-to-be. His brides couldn't be weak—he wouldn't allow it. Only the top would survive, earn their spot as one of his prizes.

He liked when his twins had some variety, and that was just what he had with this new pair. The plumper one, Sammy, stood before him on the porch of the house, her wrists tied behind her back. He'd left Susie inside; Sammy would see why soon.

It was a humid day, and Sammy's beautiful red hair glimmered against the sun. But beauty wasn't enough. She refused to look at him, her hair shielding her face as she stared at her bare feet. Tears dripped down her freckled cheeks and fell to the porch.

"Now, now, don't cry," he said, his voice soothing. "I'm gonna tell you a story. Listen good—you're gonna wanna remember this one."

Sammy nodded, but still didn't look. She was showing weakness. He didn't like that.

Regardless, he pushed on. "Weakness... can sometimes look like strength, can't it?" he said. "One time, long ago, there were two sisters... not too different from you and your Susie in there. They were taken far away, stolen together... bound together by fate." He kept rocking, his chair still creaking.

Sammy dared to look now. Her eyes were so green, and the tears made them look like emeralds.

"You see, these girls; they were taken, but they didn't stick together. No... one of them got away." He rested his hands on his belly, leaning back in the rocker. "One of them was weak. Left her sister all alone... isn't that just a shame, Sammy?"

Lip trembling, Sammy nodded.

"Well," he continued, "as the one sister saved herself... the sister she'd left behind, well. Who knows what became of her?"

"D-do you know?" Sammy asked. Her voice was so shaky, he could barely understand her.

He laughed at her question. "Do I know? *Det er lige meget...*"

Sammy blinked. She had no idea what he was saying. That was fine; it was his native tongue, but he rarely used it. Here in America, he blended in just fine; he'd spent years creating his persona, and now nobody even knew he was from another country. Good. His native tongue, his true tongue, was only for the special ones.

"W-what do you want with us?" Sammy asked.

She was getting braver. He liked that.

"I'm gonna have me some fun, Sammy," he said, laughing. "But you, though…" He sighed. "You need a lesson in what happens when you're weak."

He whistled and stood up. Sammy trembled. He brandished a knife—and Sammy's eyes went wide. "No, please, no—"

He laughed as he saw the terror in her eyes. "Oh, Sammy, don't be scared," he said, brandishing the knife. "This is just a little lesson."

He cut through her restraints with the knife, and she flinched as the blade nicked her skin. "Now, Sammy," he said, leaning close to her. "Listen to me carefully, and choose wisely."

"O-okay," she managed.

He pointed to the forest behind them with the knife. "You can go, sweetheart. You're free. Run, run, run, Sammy, and never look back…"

Sammy stiffened. She looked like she was about to bolt.

"But if you do that…" He smiled, feeing satisfied. "If you run away and come back with police…if you run away and don't come back at all…"

He pointed the knife toward the homestead.

"Then little Susie in there will get this bad boy sliced right across her throat."

Sammy's eyes went wide. "You'll kill my sister?"

"That's right, Sammy. I'll kill your sister."

Sammy stared at him, terror in her eyes. She knew he was serious. If she ran away, her sister would die. And if she came back with the police, he would kill her too. There was no way out.

He smiled at her and motioned with the knife for her to stand up. "Now, Sammy," he said softly. "It's time to choose."

She looked up at him, her green eyes shining with unshed tears. "I-I…" she began.

"Shh, Sammy," he said, leaning closer. He let his hand brush against her cheek. "There's no need to be scared."

"I-I want to run away," she whispered.

"Oh, I know you do, Sammy," he said, smiling. "But if you do… Susie will die."

Her lip began to quiver. "But I—"

"Do you want your sister to die?"

"N-no… please… don't…"

He laughed softly. "So you want to run?"

She shook her head. "I'll come home… I'll… I'll stay…"

He smiled. "Oh, that's great news, Sammy. That's just great." He placed a hand on her shoulder and squeezed. "Looks like you're one of the strong ones after all."

CHAPTER NINE

Outside of the police station, Nicky felt like her lungs were going to collapse. Yancy Rosen—he'd said Rosie's name. Whoever he saw in that bar...

He had a thing for twins. A thing for sisters.

Nicky and Rosie weren't twins, but they always did look alike. He could have mistaken them for twins. Nicky's mind spun like she was on a defunct fair ride, turning over and over again.

This person Yancy was talking about. He could be the guy Nicky had been looking for since she was sixteen.

No, she told herself. No, it can't be. All the way out here? There's no way...

Suddenly, the doors to the police station burst open, and Ken came out. The afternoon sun shone on his black hair as he rushed up to her. "Lyons, are you okay?" he asked.

Nicky shook her head. Her vision was starting to go blurry around the edges. The tears were coming. She'd barely be able to tell him what happened at all.

"What happened?"

Her mind was spinning. "He... he said the name Rosie. I mean, my sister's name. Rosie."

He blinked, looking confused. "Lyons..."

"The name Rosie. He said the name Rosie."

"Come on, let's sit down," Ken said, leading her to a bench. He sat down next to her. "You look like you're about to pass out."

Nicky relaxed against the hard plastic of the bench. What was she thinking?

"Look, I know this is a tough topic," Ken said. "But Yancy—if he said your sister's name, he's clearly messing with you. I mean, maybe he recognized you from the news. Your sister's case gained a good amount of public exposure, right?"

A lump formed in her throat. "But it's been over a decade since anything about Rosie was actually on mainstream news," she said. At the same time, Ken was making sense. "Maybe he did just recognize me from the news…"

"Listen, Lyons," Ken said. His eyes met hers sternly. "I'm gonna say something and I don't want you to react like I'm wrong or something… okay?"

She nodded. It still felt weird being comforted by Ken.

"Yancy is messing with you," Ken said. "He's trying to get you upset. I really don't think he meant anything by it."

"But—"

"Lyons, he's trying to throw you off. Remember, this is a guy who gets kicks out of making women uncomfortable," Ken reminded her. "The words of a creep are not exactly the greatest source of truth."

Nicky laughed. Ken was making sense, but when it came to Rosie… all bets were off for Nicky. She'd talked to Dr. Graham, her therapist, about it a million times, but still, real progress was never really made. Nicky still had PTSD from the event; it would never go away. Just hearing Rosie's voice had triggered her beyond belief. How could these random South Florida people have anything to do with Rosie, who'd disappeared in West Virginia so many years ago?

She needed to keep it together. Although part of her did want to ask more, just to be safe, she needed to not jump to conclusions.

"You're right," she said softly. "Yancy is just trying to mess with me. Trying to make me give up. I do still want to go in after him."

Ken shrugged. "Even so, that doesn't mean he had anything to do with your sister. You might be able to follow up on that lead, sure, but I really want you to focus on the Yancy Rosen case," he said. "That's where we're getting real, tangible results."

"Okay," Nicky managed.

"And maybe that'll help you a little bit," he added. "Correct?"

Nicky nodded. "Yeah," she said. "That helps a lot."

"So," he said. He grabbed her shoulder and squeezed. "Are you okay to go back inside?"

She shrugged. "Yeah, I'm okay…" she said. She tried not to think about it. She had to focus on the Yancy Rosen case. The Rosie case was something else, something to be dealt with at a separate time.

For now, she needed to get back in there and deal with Yancy.

***

41

Nicky breezed through the door of the interrogation room, Ken behind her. Yancy snapped to attention, looking up at them like a guilty dog. Did this guy really recognize her from the news? Was he actually capable of messing with her like that? Or maybe mentioning Rosie's name had been purely a coincidence. Many people in the US were named that, after all.

But still. It all felt off.

"Apologies for that, Yancy," Nicky said, taking her seat. "I had an important call."

Ken sat next to her. "Let's continue. Where were we…"

Nicky cut in: "The man you saw at the bar, who talked about liking the 'single twins.' What did he look like?"

"He was a tall guy. Six four, six five. Had a military buzz cut. Blue eyes. A tattoo under his shirt, a dagger or something like that."

She looked over at Ken, who quickly jotted it down. A tall, military man. That could mean anything. But the tattoo—that could give them something to work off.

But Nicky couldn't ignore the fact that the person Yancy was describing sounded nothing like the man who'd taken her and Rosie all those years ago. That man had been… sickly, and quite thin, despite his strength. Nicky couldn't remember any tattoos on him. Of course, he could have gained weight and added them over the years, but the height was another thing; she did not remember him being tall.

Refocusing on the interview, she said, "What did he wear?"

"What do you mean?" Yancy asked.

"What kind of clothes?" she asked. "And what color was the shirt?"

"He was wearing a black shirt with a skull on it. The pants were… I can't remember," Yancy said. "Maybe they were cargo pants? It was a long time ago. His friend was like a skinnier version of him, I think he had a long ponytail though."

Nicky wrote it all down. This Yancy sounded surprisingly honest… but that also meant every bit of his story might be true.

"And how did he act? Did he seem like a bad guy?" she asked.

"Kind of," Yancy replied. "He was kind of a thug. He got into a fight with a couple people in the bar. The bouncer had to kick him out."

"Any idea what he wanted with the girls? Did it seem like he wanted to kidnap people?" Ken asked.

"Well, I don't know about that," Yancy said. "That's a pretty big accusation."

42

Nicky looked at Ken, and he nodded. This "other person" was compelling, but it was time for Nicky to reveal the real reason why Yancy was brought in.

"Yancy," Nicky said, "did you hear about the two girls who went missing in the area?" When he blinked, clueless, Nicky said, "Susie and Sammy Miller. Twins. The whole community and police force were looking for them, over by the cottages."

"I don't watch the news," Yancy said. Nicky winced. If he didn't watch the news, then…

No. She shook that thought away. Focus on the task at hand, Lyons.

"Where were you three nights ago, Yancy?"

He thought for a few moments. "Well, it was real muddy out from the storm, and Joe—that's the farmer I do work for—didn't want me to get stuck in the mud. I crashed on his couch."

"His name is Joe?" Ken asked.

Yancy nodded. "Joe Reacher. He's easy to find. I can write down his number…"

"And who else was there?" Nicky asked.

"His wife, Marge, I think. And maybe his son, too," Yancy said.

"And how long were you there?" Nicky asked.

"About two days. I showed up the day after the storm and the next day the weather was still pretty bad," Yancy said. "And Joe was nice enough to let me stay."

Damn. If this checked out, then Yancy really could be cleared. Nicky wasn't sure if she should believe anything he said, but at the same time, there was something very simple about him. Now that he was opening up more, she couldn't help but get the sense he was being honest. She wasn't sure what to make of his alibi, or the story he'd told about the guy at the bar. There were definitely parallels between that story and Nicky's own kidnapping, but it didn't sound like they were the same guy.

She couldn't help but feel disappointed.

There was nothing Nicky wanted more than justice for her sister. But right now, Susie and Sammy Miller needed justice too.

They could still be alive out there. And it was up to Nicky to find them.

43

CHAPTER TEN

Back at the motel, Nicky sat at the table in the blue glow of her laptop, which she had opened in front of her. Ken was out grabbing dinner. Through the curtains of the motel room, night was falling upon them like a black cloth that was draped over Florida and was being drawn across the sky by invisible hands. The shadows of trees were growing longer and darker by the second and would soon engulf them. Where had the day gone? Nicky felt like she'd blinked, and the sun was already going down. They'd made a lot less progress today than she would have liked, and it was all draining her confidence.

The bar that Yancy had described was called the Squawking Gull, and it had gone out of business a year ago. Nicky had called around, tried to find anything about a guy with a dagger tattoo, but nothing came up.

It was a dead end.

To make matters worse, Yancy's alibi had checked out; the farmer and his wife, plus their child, had vouched for him. Yancy Rosen did not kidnap Susie and Sammy Miller.

So who did?

Nicky wasn't sure where to go from here, so she was going through old case files. Anything to do with twins or missing sisters.

The police had hundreds of different unsolved murders and kidnappings that they were looking into across the country, but in this remote area of Florida, it wasn't as common. She was checking through them for anything that might link to the two missing girls, but so far, she was coming up empty.

The case of London and Paris Knight had been bordering cold for ten months. It was looking colder by the second.

Nicky tried to keep her cool, but really, her mind was racing. All she could think about was the fact that they were supposed to be out there, looking for Susie and Sammy, but instead she was sitting in a motel room.

The door to their room opened, and Ken walked in with a bag of food. He closed the door with his foot and set the bag on the table.

"Hey, find anything new?" he asked.

"Nothing yet," Nicky muttered. The smell of burgers and fries from the bag made her mouth water. She'd managed to eat a protein bar earlier, but that was it. Sometimes, on the move like this, it was hard to find time for meal breaks.

Ken opened the bag and pulled out two burgers wrapped in paper. Then he opened a packet of fries and put them in a container. "Well, I got you these," he said.

"Thanks," Nicky said, her stomach rumbling. "But I can't believe we're here. This is just crazy."

"I know," Ken said. "This is what happens when you're on a case. You go where the clues lead you. That's all we can do, right?"

Yeah, right, Nicky thought. What else are we going to do? She took her burger and bit into it, savoring the juicy meat and the crunch of the lettuce. It was a burger from a fast food joint, but it tasted great, and she could feel her energy returning.

"So, what now?" Ken asked.

"Good question. I don't know," Nicky said. She sighed and leaned back in her chair. She was feeling defeated. "I'm just gonna keep looking at case files until something comes up. There has to be something we're missing."

"Yeah, but you've been going over the same stuff for a long time. It's gotta be boring," Ken said.

"It is." Nicky took another big bite of her burger, chewed it, and swallowed. She made a face. "I can't believe we're doing this," she said.

"What's that?" Ken asked.

"This. This case. This whole thing," Nicky said. "We're supposed to be out there—"

"Looking for the girls," Ken said.

"But all we're doing is sitting here. It's not working," Nicky said. "We're not getting anywhere."

"Well, you can't expect to find them right away. We're just getting started," Ken said.

"But we have to find them before it's too late. We don't know what condition they're in," Nicky said. Her resolve burning back to life, she went on the laptop. As much as she wanted to get out on the field, she knew that sometimes, the most she could do for a victim was research. She had to find out where Susie and Sammy could be before she could actually be the hero and go out there. But still, sitting around, eating a burger… didn't make her feel good while those girls were suffering, like she and Rosie had suffered all those years ago.

Letting her fries go cold, Nicky went onto the laptop and continued looking into case files.

She read about the missing women, about how no one had heard from them in years, how their families were constantly waiting for news, for any news of their loved ones…

Her heart went out to them. It was a pain she knew all too well, but she also knew that as long as she was actively searching for Susie and Sammy, she was doing something. It wasn't much, but it was something.

Ken finished his food, then took out his own laptop.

"You tell me what you find, and I'll tell you what I find," she said to Ken, without looking at him. "And together, we can figure this out."

"Let's do it," Ken said, clacking away at his keyboard.

Minutes passed as Nicky searched case notes for anything that might stand out. She decided to look back into London and Paris Knight, the original twins on the FBI's list. Like Susie and Sammy, they'd been staying at a vacation home pretty far out in the bush when they went missing. It was a few hours from here, though, and it was near the shore of the beach. Much more lavish than Sammy and Susie's family cottage. But still, the circumstances were near identical.

Nicky flipped through notes about the case made by the detectives who were on it before it was passed down to the FBI. Interviews with witnesses were slim…

But one person, a young woman, said she thought she heard a vehicle revving late at night, the same night the women went missing.

The detective left a note theorizing that the kidnapper was getting around on something with a loud engine.

Nicky paused. Hold on…

She took out her phone, pulling up the picture she'd taken at the crime scene of what looked like two partings in the grass. It could be from wheels, although any tire tracks were washed away in the rain. But these two spaces, damage to the grass, were fairly uniform. They could easily be from some sort of off-road vehicle, which would explain how he was able to get around in such bad conditions.

He probably had a vehicle capable of handling it.

Nicky's heart pounded. She was onto something here.

She thought back to the child from last night. The little boy who said he'd heard a monster growling.

Maybe it wasn't a monster or an animal at all.

Maybe it was the sound of an engine.

Nicky turned to Ken. "I think I have something here," she said.

"What?" Ken asked. He looked up from his laptop.

"I think it's a vehicle. Maybe a car. Maybe an ATV. Maybe something else. I'm not sure," Nicky said.

"How's an ATV going to help him take the girls? It would've been hard to drive through all that mud," Ken said.

"He could have modified wheels. Or maybe it was a Jeep. It says right here that before London and Paris went missing, a witness thought she heard a loud engine."

Ken nodded, the realization dawning on his face. "And that little kid..."

"He heard a noise too."

Pulse in her throat, Nicky went online. She found a website that could play different engine sounds, and she played them all.

Nicky cocked her head, listening. She closed her eyes, focusing, and heard the simple and unmistakable sound of a vehicle. She recognized it.

It was a powerful ATV. One that could go through mud and water and still get around. She pulled up a video of a Jeep Wrangler driving, and the engine roared as loud as a lion's growl.

Nicky looked up at Ken. "One of these could be what the boy heard. An off-road vehicle."

"It's possible," Ken said.

Very possible. In fact, the more Nicky thought on it, the more certain she felt.

This was a major clue. If they could identify the sound of the vehicle, they may be able to identify the mode—which could lead them straight to the kidnapper. Nicky didn't want to get ahead of herself, but this felt huge.

"It's just a theory right now," she said. "But I think it's worth a shot to get out there." She stood up.

"Get out where?" Ken asked, standing too.

Nicky slammed the laptop shut. "I think we need to go talk to that little boy again."

CHAPTER ELEVEN

Nicky pulled her car up in front of the cottage where the little boy, Jacob, was staying with his family. They had tried to call ahead, but no one answered the phone. There was a car parked in the driveway, though, and inside, the lights were on. It was dark out, nearly black so far away from city lights. The tire swing on the tree slowly swayed in the breeze.

Nicky put the car in park and faced Ken, who looked uncertain. "I don't know about this, Lyons," he said. "He's just a kid, and if the parents weren't answering our calls…"

"It doesn't matter," Nicky said. "We need to talk to him."

"I just don't know if it will prove anything." Ken ran a hand through his black hair. "I mean, the kid thought the sound was a monster… how credible is his statement, really?"

"Well, we're not investigating monsters right now, are we? And we never know what will turn out to be useful," Nicky said.

"Okay," Ken said, taking in a breath. "But let's just be gentle."

"I know," Nicky said. "We can't know unless we talk to him. If he heard something that could be a vehicle, we need to find out; he can help identify the make."

"Okay," Ken breathed out. "You're the boss."

They got out of the car and walked up the path and onto the front porch. Both hesitated, looking at each other, before Nicky knocked. A long pause happened before Nicky heard movement on the other side of the door—maybe even whispering. Emboldened, she knocked again.

This time, the young mother she had met just yesterday poked her head out, looking at the two FBI agents warily.

"Hi, Ms. Walker?" Nicky asked. "We met yesterday."

"Oh, yes…" She cleared her throat. "Please call me Claire."

"We tried calling," Nicky said, "but there was no answer."

The smell of pasta wafted out from inside. "We were just having dinner," Claire said, but Nicky got the sense she was being dishonest. She wouldn't fully open the door to let them see inside.

"We're here to talk to Jacob again," Nicky said.

48

Claire hesitated for a moment, looking back into the cottage. "Jacob is sleeping," she said. "Can you come back tomorrow?"

Nicky was about to respond when a child's voice—Jacob's voice—sounded from inside. "Mom!" he yelled.

Claire flinched and looked back in the house, then shot a guilty look at Nicky and Ken. "Look," Claire said, "Jacob… he's not well, okay? Whatever he thinks he heard, plus the girls going missing, has made him extremely anxious. Talking to the FBI is only going to hurt him."

"I'm sorry to do this, Claire," Nicky said. "It brings us no pleasure, but this is a serious criminal investigation, and your son may have witnessed something crucial to our case."

"I don't think he'll be talkative," Claire said. "He's been getting worse."

"We really need to talk to him," Nicky said. "We need him to listen to a few recordings of automobiles to help us identify what the kidnapper may have been driving."

Claire looked back in the house again, then at the agents. "You think that's what the noise was? A car?"

"Something like that," Nicky said. "We certainly don't want to harm your son, but Susie and Sammy Miller are missing, and someone took them. We need to know who."

Claire bit her lip, glancing back into the house. Nicky hoped she'd make the right decision. She understood Claire's desire to protect her child, but at the same time, somebody else's children were in critical danger—or worse.

"Fine," Claire said finally. She sighed. "Come in."

Relief flowed through Nicky. Claire led Nicky and Ken down the hallway, past the bedrooms and into the living room. A coffee table sat in the middle of the dark, worn hardwood floor. It was surrounded by a red leather recliner, a couch, and two chairs. Claire sat on one of the chairs, which was made of an oversized foam material that looked comfortable. Nicky and Ken sat on opposite sides of the couch. The musty, yet comforting smell of the cottage surrounded them.

"Jacob!" Claire called.

Moments later, the little boy came running down the stairs. He stopped short, looking at the two FBI agents, then his mother. "What's going on?" he asked, fear in his voice. "Is something wrong?"

"No, no, Jacob," Claire said, although her voice shook. "Nothing is wrong, honey. They're just here to ask you a few questions again, okay?"

"Okay…" Jacob glanced at Nicky and Ken.

"Jacob?" Nicky asked. "Do you remember me?"

He nodded. "You're the lady from yesterday!"

"That's right," she said. "Do you remember what we talked about before?"

"Yes."

"Can you tell me again what you heard?" Nicky asked.

Jacob's eyes went wide, and he looked around, as if he might see someone behind him. "No," he said. "Mom told me not to talk about it."

"Jacob…" Nicky said, her voice going soft and gentle. "We just want to help find the people who took Susie and Sammy. If you help us, we can stop that from happening again."

Jacob nodded, but he didn't look convinced.

"You say you heard a monster," Ken said. His voice was gentle. "That's why you were afraid of the noise?"

"Um, yeah," Jacob said.

"Do you know what kind of monster it was?" Ken asked. "Big? Like a dinosaur?"

Jacob shook his head.

"What kind of monster sounds like what you heard?" Nicky asked.

Jacob scrunched up his face. He looked like he was concentrating hard. "A great big bear, maybe."

"Well, there are no bears out here," Nicky said. "What if I told you the sound didn't come from a monster at all? Maybe it was just from a car, or some other type of automobile. You like cars, right?" Nicky said, taking note of the toybox across the room, which had a bunch of toy cars beside it.

Jacob nodded, still looking scared. He glanced at the agents. "That wouldn't be so scary."

"That's right," Nicky said. She smiled at him. "We just have some recordings we'd like you to listen to."

Jacob's forehead creased. "Recording? What recording?"

"They're not monsters. They're just cars. Is that okay, Jacob?"

Hesitantly, he nodded, biting down on his thumb.

Nicky slipped her laptop out of her bag, then turned it on and waited for it to boot up. Claire looked at Nicky, worried, but she and Ken stayed silent. They knew the kid was scared enough.

A few seconds later, Nicky started the Windows Media Player, then opened the file she had created earlier. "Jacob, would you come over here?" she asked, patting the couch next to her.

Jacob stood, hesitated, then cautiously walked over and sat down next to Nicky. Nicky set the laptop on the couch between them. A second later, the roar of a powerful engine filled the cottage. This was the Jeep, the one Nicky was most certain the kidnapper could have used.

"Is that what you heard, Jacob?" Nicky asked.

He shook his head. "I don't think so…"

"Let me play the next one," Nicky said. She fast-forwarded to the next file, where the car growled, then revved loudly, the engine roaring.

Jacob's face went pale and his eyes widened. He shook his head. "No, that's not it," he said. "That car is quieter."

"How about this one?" Nicky asked, playing the next sample.

Again, Jacob shook his head, his face even more pale.

Nicky kept playing the samples, until they got down to the last few, but Jacob was still shaking his head. He started to get more and more upset, but the agents were almost done. Nicky went through all the samples, making sure to play the truck, the motorcycle, and even the boat. Jacob just kept shaking his head. Finally, Nicky played the final one—the ATV—and Jacob stiffened.

The ATV engine growled again. This time, Jacob's eyes went wide. Nicky's pulse raced. She glanced at Ken, whose brow was furrowed.

"It was this one, wasn't it, Jacob?" Nicky asked.

Claire came over and wrapped an arm around Jacob. "It's okay, sweetie. Tell the agents what you remember."

Jacob met Nicky's eyes. "Yes," he said, his voice trembling. "It was this one. It was loud, like the monster I saw."

Nicky blinked, surprised. She and Ken looked at each other, then back to Jacob. "You saw a monster?"

He shook his head. "No. I didn't see it. But I heard it. It was loud and growly, like that. It made me scared."

Nicky and Ken looked at each other again, this time surprised at seeing the same shocked look on both their faces.

"Jacob, is there anything else you can remember?" Nicky asked. "Anything you remember about the monster that sounds like a car?"

Claire tensed up, but Jacob kept his eyes on Nicky. "I heard it roaring. It was loud. And it made me very scared."

"This is the sound of an ATV, Jacob," Nicky said.

Jacob was shaking his head, but then the engine revved again, and he looked up at his mother, then at Nicky. "It was this one," he said in a small voice.

"Are you sure?" Nicky asked.

He nodded. "I'm sure."

Nicky's heart thundered. She looked at Ken, and Ken looked at her. This was their only lead—and Jacob had just strengthened it. She couldn't believe it.

Jacob had gone back to Claire. Claire sat him down on the chair and pulled his legs up, then sat down next to him. Jacob was looking down at the floor, his eyes wide and teary.

"I'm sorry, honey," Claire said, brushing strands of red-blond hair off Jacob's cheek. "I'm sorry they have to put you through this."

"That's okay, Mom," Jacob said.

Claire nuzzled next to him. "You're a real trouper, Jacob."

He smiled. "I try."

"I know you do," Claire said. She kissed him on the forehead, then stood, facing Nicky and Ken. "Do you have everything you need?"

Nicky nodded. "We do. If you need to talk to us again, we're going to be in the area, so…"

"I'll call you," Claire said. "Don't worry."

"We're so sorry to put your son through this," Ken said. "I'm sure you don't need to hear that, but we are."

"I know," Claire said. "You're just doing your jobs."

"Well, thank you for being so understanding," Ken said.

"Of course," Claire said.

Nicky and Ken collected their things and then headed outside, where Nicky's car was parked. Nicky got in, and Ken went around to the other side. Nicky watched him get in, then looked out the window at the cottage. She could see Jacob standing at the window, watching them. He waved, and Nicky waved back.

This little boy had helped them more than he could know. Because now, they weren't just looking for a kidnapper.

52

They were looking for a kidnapper with an ATV. And that would narrow down their search considerably.

CHAPTER TWELVE

The fan in the motel room hummed as Nicky and Ken walked through the door. This time, Nicky had a clearer goal in mind: to discover any incidents involving an ATV in the area. This new break was huge, and Nicky felt the familiar thrill of excitement as she sat down at the table, pulling her laptop out. The motel's Wi-Fi was shoddy, but it would do.

"Ready?" Nicky asked Ken as she logged into her laptop.

Ken eased into the chair across from her, stifling a yawn. "I need more coffee, but damn right I'm ready."

"That's the spirit, Walker."

Ken grinned at her, then grabbed his notebook, scribbling something down as Nicky got to work. She opened the files for the U.S. Forest Service and spent a good forty-five minutes going through them. She checked for incidents in the area that might be related, but found nothing that matched her parameters.

Nicky opened Google, then started a new search, looking for "ATV incident, Southern Florida" and hitting enter. A list of results appeared, from local news stations to blogs, and Nicky started reading, looking for any leads that might match what had happened here.

The more she read, the more her excitement grew. She read about ATV accidents, ATV thefts, ATV sales, ATV races—but no kidnappings involving ATVs. Her excitement turned to disappointment, and then to irritation.

She started a new search, this time adding the word "kidnapped" to the search string, then she hit enter.

The results were huge, but Nicky quickly narrowed them down by adding South Florida to the search. The results were still huge, but she started reading, trying to find any leads that might match what happened here.

She'd found two incidents that looked like they might be related, but when she checked the dates and locations, she found they didn't match. One went back to 1960. The most recent incident had happened over a thousand miles away, and the older one was almost a thousand miles away, too.

Maybe this was the wrong thing. Nicky hated the idea that the ATV lead would go nowhere. She had to dig deeper. Maybe looking online wasn't enough; there could be something that never made it to mainstream news.

So, she went into the FBI database.

Nicky signed into the database, then started looking. She went back to the time of the kidnapping and searched for any ATV incidents, then looked at the statistics of those incidents. She wanted to see if there were any patterns, anything that would lead to what she was looking for.

The more she read, the more her frustration grew.

"No luck?" Ken asked.

Nicky kept scrolling through case files. "Nothing that seems related yet, but I'm not done." And she wouldn't be, not until she found something she could use.

Just then, Nicky's phone buzzed in her pocket. She took it out to see there was a text from Matt. As soon as she saw his name, her stomach dropped. She had barely even thought about him since their date ended.

Matt: Hey, I haven't heard from ya! Hope I didn't scare you off…

One of the major things Dr. Graham, Nicky's psychiatrist, wanted her to work on was letting people in. Not just coworkers—actual friends, whom she could see outside of work, whom she could rely on. Matt seemed like a safe bet, but still, Nicky wasn't used to having someone to text. When she had a thing with Fernando, her coworker at the office, it had been easy business; they didn't text, they just saw each other in person, and sometimes he'd come to her place after work. But Nicky had ended that a long time ago. Part of her had given up on the idea of having a relationship that was more than just sex.

But Matt—he was her childhood friend. He was a good guy. She had to make time for him, even a little; she didn't want him to think she was ghosting him.

Nicky took a moment to text back: Sorry, I'm working a case. We'll make plans soon, okay?

She even added a heart emoji to sweeten the deal. Hopefully that would be enough for now.

Across the table, Ken lifted an eyebrow. "Who are you texting?"

Nicky felt her face flush, and she put the phone away. "Ah, just a friend."

"You have friends?" Ken teased. "How shocking."

"Oh, ha ha," Nicky said. "This friend in particular is very important to me."

She was being a little facetious, but there was a kernel of truth there. Matt was important to her, especially because they had been friends since they were kids. Maybe she hadn't seen it that way before, but she did now. Maybe it was time to work on making it a more adult friendship, the way she was supposed to.

"I'm just teasing, Nicky," Ken said. "I'm glad you've got friends. I almost took you for a loner."

"Says the man who won't tell me anything about his personal life," Nicky said. "Believe it or not, I'm fun at parties. I'd drink you under the table, Walker. But you haven't been in the office long enough to see me at a work event."

"You get drunk at work parties?"

Nicky winked. "Only outside of office hours."

Ken laughed and shook his head. "Now that's something I need to see."

"I'm just kidding," Nicky said. "No drinking around the boss." She pretended to pick up a cup and cheer the air. "Franco's no fun at work events anyway, he's too serious. I've had a few drinks with coworkers outside of office hours, though." Nicky paused. "You should come sometime."

Ken looked down at his laptop, and it lit his stern features. He had thick black eyelashes and the bluest eyes Nicky had ever seen, illuminated by the screen. "I don't have time for fun, Lyons."

"Me neither," Nicky said, "not on a case. But sometimes when you get a really good win... it's nice to unwind."

Ken said nothing, and Nicky was reminded that she really knew nothing about him. They'd barely been partners for two weeks, but still. The most Nicky knew about him was that his girlfriend in high school was kidnapped and murdered, which motivated him to become an FBI agent. She wondered if Ken would be a fun guy if that had never happened to him.

Brushing that aside, Nicky refocused on her computer. She'd gotten sidetracked, but she geared herself back to her mission: finding a link between a crime involving an ATV, and what happened to Susie and Sammy.

There were dozens of hits, from theft reports to arrests to… a hit.

Wait a second…

Nicky opened a file, her heart in her throat. It was ten years old, but it clearly stated that there was a man who drove an ATV around and harassed women.

One time, he picked up a couple of hitchhikers—two eighteen-year-old girls—and sexually assaulted them. The victims were not twins, but they were still young girls. And all of this had happened not far from the cottages where the twins went missing.

Nicky's heart thundered. Was this it?

She called up the file and then started reading.

She read about the man's habits, the way he approached his victims. He picked up hitchhikers, then ordered them to strip. He ordered one girl out of the car, and then he abducted her, but she was able to get away.

The other girl was taken, and then she was found, her clothes discarded in a pile near the ATV.

The mother of the girl who was abducted said she was sure that the man who took her daughter was the same man who had been harassing women in the area.

The description the mother gave was vague at best, but there was a sketch, and the sketch looked like it could be a match to the man they had in custody at the time.

The name of the man was Jerry Bocanegra.

And he'd gotten out of prison eleven months ago—just one month before London and Paris Knight went missing.

"Holy…" Nicky took a breath. "Walker, you need to see this."

"What?" Ken said.

"I've got a hit," Nicky said. "I think… I think we've got him."

Ken's eyes widened. "What?"

Nicky opened a new tab and started a new search. She typed in the name Jerry Bocanegra, then started looking for any information she could find on him.

She found his mugshot, as well as a police report with Jerry's name and his description.

She saw the sketch of what the mother of the girl who had been abducted by Jerry remembered him looking like. It was hard to tell whether the sketch matched Jerry, or whether the mother just made a mistake, but that sketch definitely looked like the suspect they had in custody.

"Jesus, Lyons, don't leave me hanging here," Ken said. "Let me see."

"Sorry, here." Nicky handed him the laptop, watching as he read the information.

When he finished, he looked up. "That could be our guy."

"I think it is," Nicky said, standing up. "I think we should pay him a visit."

CHAPTER THIRTEEN

The headlights of Nicky's car cut through the night. Navigating this backcountry terrain was even more treacherous without daylight, and she kept her high beams on, trying not to let Ken know she was nervous. Nicky rarely, if ever, relinquished control of the wheel. Being a passenger was not her style. Not after she and Rosie had been kidnapped and thrown in the back of someone's van all those years ago. Ever since then, Nicky had hated being anywhere but behind the wheel.

Still, with the way the tires were bumping off every rock, she was nervous. Driving through the darkness, like a beam of light slicing through pure black, made her oddly paranoid.

They were on their way to Jerry Bocanegra's address, which unsurprisingly was a good drive from the cottages, but it wasn't as backwoods as Yancy's, and the GPS said they would be arriving soon. Nicky wasn't looking forward to getting to know a guy who'd been locked up for nearly ten years and was now released back into the wild. Maybe he was even the one who'd taken the girls.

"Do you think he'll talk to us?" Ken said, filling the silence in the dark car.

Nicky shrugged. "I don't know. I have a feeling we'd get more out of him if we let him think we know more than we do."

"Yeah, well, that's the problem," Ken said. "We don't have enough for an arrest."

"We don't have enough yet," Nicky said. "But I have a feeling he's going to slip up."

As Nicky drove, she couldn't help but think back to when she and Rosie had been kidnapped. When Nicky had managed to escape, it was a night like this; warm, dark, slightly humid. She hated the way those memories were buried so deep within her, yet always at the surface. She was sure they'd never go away until she found Rosie alive.

"Psychopaths rarely change," Nicky said absently. "This Jerry guy spent ten years in prison. Maybe now that he's out, he's right back to his old ways."

"Yeah," Ken said. "Maybe he was biding his time before he got out."

Nicky slowed down a little as she turned around a curve in the dirt road. The tires bumped off a rock and she tensed, gripping the wheel harder.

"Maybe he's already taken more girls, and we don't even know about it," Nicky said. "Maybe he's picking off hitchhikers, or people in campgrounds, or getting them from rooms he's rented in cottages. He could be luring them in, keeping them somewhere, and using them when he wants."

"So you think they're still alive?" Ken asked.

Nicky gripped the steering wheel, her knuckles going white. "I hope so, Walker."

Finally, they pulled up outside of the farmhouse Jerry lived in. There was nothing special about the way it looked. It was a two-story farmhouse, weathered, and the paint was flaking off the wood. Weeds had grown up around the foundation and the old wooden porch, or rather the two steps leading up to it. An American flag flapped in the breeze on the flagpole. There was an old, rusted truck in the driveway, and a light on inside the house, so someone was home.

"Well, this is it," Nicky said.

"Want me to do the talking?" Ken asked.

Nicky shook her head. "I've got it. You just stay close."

"Always do," Ken said.

Nicky climbed out of the car and walked up the steps to the porch. She rang the doorbell, and they waited in the hot silence.

"I'm not sure he's even here," Ken said.

"He's here," Nicky said. "He has to be."

Nicky rang the doorbell a few more times, and then she stood back, arms crossed.

Finally, something sounded on the other side—a cough.

A skinny, twenty-something guy answered the door. He was wearing a denim vest and pajamas and had stick and poke tattoos all over his arms. When he saw Nicky and Ken, he frowned.

This was definitely not Jerry Bocanegra, who was visibly heavyset in his pictures.

"Who the hell are you?" the guy asked.

Nicky held up her badge, and Ken did too. The guy's face went pale.

"I'm Agent Nicky Lyons of the FBI, and this is my partner, Agent Ken Walker. We're looking for Jerry Bocanegra."

"Uh, I'm his brother… name's James."

"Is Jerry home, James?"

"He's not here," James said.

Nicky didn't buy it. "Are you sure about that?"

"Really," James said. "He's not. I wouldn't lie. No reason to protect him."

"Can we come in?" Nicky asked.

James shrugged, opening the door for them. "Sure, I guess…"

Nicky looked around at the living room of the farmhouse. It was a mess. Canned food and takeout bags littered the coffee table. The couch was covered in dirty clothes, and empty beer bottles were everywhere.

"Jerry went hunting," James said. "He's been gone for a few days."

Of course he'd be out doing something like that. "Where did he go?" Nicky asked.

"Into the woods," James said. "Probably to our family's old hunting cabin. Has he done something again?"

Clearly, the family was used to this guy and his illegal activities. Nicky wasn't surprised. "We just need to speak to him," Nicky said. "Do you have any idea when he'll be back?"

"No, I don't know. Soon, I guess. He goes into the woods for a few days at a time, lots of times."

"So he does this often?" Ken asked.

"Yeah, he has been for years, or had been before he went to the clink," James said. "He used to take me fishing up at the lake. He'd always kill a deer and bring one of 'em home."

"When was the last time you saw him?"

"Yesterday," James said. "At like, eleven in the morning. He came back, took a shower, and left again. The rest of the day, I didn't see him."

"Why did he come back?" Ken asked.

"To get some clothes," James said. "And to get his gun. He's got a lot of guns, locked in the top drawer of his dresser. I'm not supposed to touch them."

Nicky shared a look with Ken and instinctively felt for her gun, strapped on her belt under her jacket. So, not only was Jerry potentially their target—but he was armed. This wasn't good.

61

"Jer was gone for ten years," James continued, "but you'd never tell… when he got home from prison, it was like he just waltzed back into the life he'd always lived." He cleared his throat. "Listen, I'm not here to protect him. If he's doing illegal stuff again, count me out. I just got off probation myself, and I'm cleaning my act up."

"How did Jerry get home?" Ken asked.

"I picked him up from prison myself," James said. "I never would've done it if I hadn't caught him in a lie. He told me he was being let out early for good behavior. He said there was a clerical error and someone else had to stay in longer than him."

"What was the lie?" Ken asked.

"That he was going to get a job and be straight," James said. "He was going to get a job at a warehouse, and he had all these plans and shit, but he just stays in his room when he's not hunting. I don't even think he's looking for a job."

Nicky nodded. For now, they had enough. But one thing remained: "Do you have directions to this hunting cabin?"

James nodded. "Follow me."

Ken and Nicky followed him out of the house and into the driveway. He walked over to a beat up old truck with a cracked windshield.

He opened the door and rooted around inside, throwing blankets, books, and a few beers onto the lawn. Finally, he reached into the glove compartment and pulled out a folded up map. He handed it to Nicky, who opened it and studied it.

"We're here, right?" Nicky asked, pointing to the red dot.

"Yeah," James said. "Right at the intersection of the road into the hunting cabin."

"What's the cabin's address?" Ken asked.

"Ah, let me see," James said, digging around in the glove compartment again. "Here it is." He handed Ken a slip of paper, and Ken glanced at it.

"Thanks," Nicky said.

"I'll tell you guys one thing," James said. "My brother's a good shot. He always was…"

"What's that?" Ken asked.

"He always had a knack for it," James said. "When we were kids, I'd be out hunting for squirrels, and I'd see him hunched down, aiming his gun at a tree, only he wasn't banding his arm or anything. He wasn't even sweating. He'd shoot and kill a squirrel. With his first shot." James licked his lips. "He was a good shot. He still is."

Nicky's heart felt heavy. There was a stillness in the night—a finality. She didn't like the sound of this Jerry guy, and she had a bad feeling about all of this. Something in her gut was telling her they should wait until morning...

But this hunting cabin—it could be where Jerry was keeping the girls if he had them. And Nicky couldn't wait around all night and let him torture them more—or worse.

They had to go now.

"Thanks, James," Nicky said. "You've been very helpful."

With that, the agents walked away, and Nicky touched the back of her gun again as she made her way back to the car. She looked at Ken, who nodded at her, a certain apprehension in his blue eyes. They were thinking the same thing.

They were going after this guy. But they hoped they weren't about to make a fatal mistake.

CHAPTER FOURTEEN

Nicky parked the car at the edge of the woods, just before the road to the hunting cabin. It was less than a half moon that night, and the sky was clear and cloudless, but the moonlight was soft, the darkness in between the trunks of the pines like deep shadows.

The cabin was close by. Nicky could hear the light chirping of crickets, and she could feel the energy from the forest—the energy of the animals that lived in these woods. Her heart beat fast. It was midnight, and her anticipation for what lay inside the cabin was unbearable. But had they waited too long? Had Jerry already left for the night?

Ken looked at the directions James had given them, and he checked them over a few times. He switched on the flashlight and shone it on the paper. "Looks like we go in about half a mile, and then there will be a clearing on the right, and we'll see it."

"Yeah," Nicky said. She reached for her gun and checked it briefly, making sure it was loaded. "Let's go."

They got out of the car. Ken closed the door and locked it, and they started through the woods.

"You still think this is a good idea?" Ken asked.

"Yeah," Nicky said. "I do. We can't take any chances. We have to go after them—waiting around could mean life or death for those girls."

Ken stopped and turned to face her. "Listen," he said. "If that is Jerry's cabin and if he hurts those girls, if he hurts them bad, he might kill them. We can't go in there with guns blazing. We need to be smart. Jerry could be an animal, and I don't think he'll hesitate to shoot."

Nicky nodded. Ken's words were sobering. "I'm thinking the same thing, Walker. Don't worry. I'm not taking this lightly."

They started through the woods again, and as they walked, Nicky studied the woods. This place didn't seem like it had been visited all that much. There was no evidence of any paths being worn through the underbrush here, and definitely no sign of any structures. It was as if no one had ever been here…

But Jerry had been here. People had been here, and recently. The question was, was Jerry here with these girls, or had he left them locked up somewhere else, under the watchful eye of one of his friends?

"I don't see any signs of a cabin," Ken said. He shone the flashlight around, looking for something, anything. "This is bullshit."

"Wait," Nicky said. She stopped, and Ken stopped also. The sound of trickling water danced through the air. According to the brother's directions, the cabin was near a stream. "I hear water," Nicky said.

"You do?" Ken asked.

"Yeah," Nicky said. "There. Listen."

Ken stood still, listening. He nodded. "I hear it too. This way."

They moved onward, and as they did, Nicky felt her heart beat faster. She prayed she wasn't leading Ken into a death trap. What if Jerry was lying in wait, armed with a gun and ready to shoot them? What if they were walking straight into the hands of a serial killer, who just so happened to be armed?

Nicky and Ken kept moving, and after a few more minutes, they reached the clearing. The moonlight was bright and it made for easy walking. The forest canopy was thick and blocked most of the moonlight, but it was bright enough to see.

They walked forward, and sure enough, there was the cabin.

It was a one-story building, with a rusted tin roof. It looked like the kind of cabin a bear might build from a set of wooden blocks. Or maybe it was the kind of cabin a dog might build from a pile of sticks. Either way, the structure didn't look like much. It was a long, narrow structure, with a front porch on one side and a back porch on the other. There were windows with curtains, but they were closed—and there were no lights on inside.

Ken and Nicky crept forward. They walked slowly, carefully, making sure to avoid stepping on any branches or leaves that might crunch beneath their feet. Nicky's heart was beating fast, and she knew this was probably going to be a very bad decision. But she was determined to do what she had to do.

"I don't see any cars," Nicky said.

"Neither do I," Ken said.

"That's weird," Nicky said. "His brother said he drove here."

"Maybe he parked somewhere else," Ken said.

Nicky nodded. "We should see if there are any tire tracks."

"Good idea," Ken said. They surveyed the ground in front of the cabin. A lot of dust had built up over time, and there were a lot of leaves that had probably fallen off the trees in the fall, but there was no sign of any tire tracks. Nicky frowned.

"What is it?" Ken asked.

"No tracks," Nicky said.

"What does that mean?"

"I don't know. It just doesn't look right."

Ken crossed his arms. He looked thoughtful for a moment, and then he nodded. "Yeah, you're right. It doesn't look right."

Nicky kept her eyes focused on the ground, until she saw it: footprints in the mud.

Fresh footprints.

Jerry had been here—recently.

"He's been here," Nicky said. "We have to be careful."

"You think he's here?" Ken whispered.

"I think he's here, and I think he's definitely armed," Nicky whispered back. "We need to be careful."

They walked slowly, carefully, over to the cabin. There were heavy wooden steps leading up to the porch, and they went up slowly, careful not to make too much noise. In the dark, the cabin looked even more like a child's construct—a kid's playhouse.

When they reached the top, Nicky paused and looked around her. Her eyes searched the darkness, her ears tuned for the slightest sound.

Nicky listened, and she heard the sound of crickets chirping wildly. Their music felt almost deafening, especially in the silence of the night air. She breathed in, and she could smell the fresh pine scent of this place. It was a heady aroma, and for a moment, she felt like she was back in the forest, walking through the woods. It was a calming sensation, and it made her feel comfortable and relaxed. But that feeling went away as soon as she saw the front door.

It was ajar, slightly raised. Nicky gulped. She looked at Ken, and she could see the tension in his expression. He was feeling it too.

They moved toward the door, approaching it carefully, slowly, and Ken held out his hand. He touched the wood a couple of times, making sure the door was ready to open without making much noise.

It was quiet, except for the crickets and the wind in the trees.

Nicky took a deep breath, trying to calm down. She took a few steps back, and Ken opened the door. He raised it slowly, watching it, making sure it didn't make too much noise. And then he opened it the rest of the way, and they went inside.

The cabin was dark, but they both had flashlights, so they shone the light around, illuminating the interior as much as they could.

The cabin was rustic and simple. A small, cozy living room sat on the right-hand side, with a kitchen on the left. Surely Jerry had been here, because the curtains in both rooms were drawn, and there was a plate on the table.

Nicky looked around and saw the place was just a normal cabin. There was a simple table, with a few chairs. There was a homey, rustic feel to the place. There were photos of animals—deer mostly—on the walls, and there was a rug on the wooden floor.

A fireplace. A couch. It was nothing like the empty cabin Nicky had been taken to all those years ago with Rosie.

"We should check the bedrooms," Nicky said. "Maybe they're back there."

Ken nodded. "Maybe."

They went back into the kitchen and walked toward the back door. It was ajar, just like the front door had been. They looked out through the windows and saw the stream, which was beautiful, twinkling in the moonlight.

Nicky prayed that she was right, that Jerry was in the cabin, and that he had the girls inside.

"This is it," Nicky said. "This is where they're going to be."

"Or he's going to be," Ken said.

"Yeah," Nicky said.

They crept up the hallway and reached the first bedroom. Nicky opened the door, and she saw it was empty. There was nothing in there at all. It was a simple bedroom, big enough for a bed and a dresser. There were no pictures on the wall. It was dark and empty. The second bedroom was just as empty.

Nicky and Ken went back into the hallway and crept toward the last room. The one with the door that was slightly ajar.

Nicky raised her gun and took a deep breath. She put her finger on the trigger and pushed gently on the door, hoping to open it without any sound at all.

But when she pushed the door, it made an awful creaking sound. It was hard to silence a door.

Nicky froze. She exchanged a glance with Ken, who nodded. With that, Nicky pushed the door fully open and stepped into the room.

The bedroom was empty.

The two of them looked around. There was nothing in the bedroom at all.

Jerry wasn't there. And neither were the missing girls.

Damn it. Nicky's fists clenched. Had they really been chasing another dead end? Jerry had seemed promising. But Nicky wasn't willing to give up. She didn't see ATV tire tracks, and Jerry could be keeping the girls elsewhere.

Then they heard it: a click.

The click of a gun. Nicky and Ken turned to face the doorway of the bedroom to see a heavyset man with a gun pointed right at them.

Jerry Bocanegra.

CHAPTER FIFTEEN

Nicky's heart stalled in her chest. She and Ken froze, and Jerry stared them down. His eyes were wide and wild, and he looked as if he'd been awake for a few days straight, staring at the walls.

He was a man crazed.

"Who the hell are you?" Jerry uttered.

Nicky had her gun pointed right back at him, but her palms were sweaty and her finger was hesitant on the trigger. If she shot, Jerry could shoot too.

She was seconds away from death.

"Jerry Bocanegra," Nicky said, keeping her voice firm. "Please lower your weapon. We're with the FBI. I'm Agent Nicky Lyons and—"

"How the hell did you find this place?" Jerry took a step deeper into the room, the gun still pointed high. Both Nicky and Ken stepped back.

"Your brother told us how to get here," Ken said. "We just wanna talk."

Jerry's nostrils flared. Only the moonlight through the window gave Nicky vision, but she could make out Jerry's deranged face. "Talk about what?"

"Why don't you put down your weapon and we can talk about it?" Nicky said. She had to find a way to disarm him before this got out of control.

"Why don't you get the hell off my property before I blow your brains out?" Jerry countered. "I just told my brother that he better keep his mouth shut, and I'll tell you the same damn thing. You wanna interrogate me? Fine. But only over a casket."

Nicky's adrenaline was pumping so hard she could barely keep herself still. She glanced at Ken and saw that he was just as rattled, if not more. But they had to do something.

Jerry took another step toward them, and Nicky saw that his hands were shaking. He had a gun in one hand and a bottle of whiskey in the other. He had to be drunk.

69

"I swear, if you don't put that down and get out of here, I'm going to shoot you!" he shouted. "I don't think you wanna see what happens when I start shooting!"

He took another step toward the doorway.

Nicky and Ken took another step back.

"We just wanna talk," Ken said. "Put down the gun."

"I don't wanna talk to you," Jerry said. "I don't wanna talk to anyone. Get the hell out of here."

Nicky shook her head. "Not until you put down the gun."

Jerry's eyes flashed, wild and furious. He seemed to be on the verge of losing his mind. "I don't want to talk to you! I don't want to talk to anyone! I just want to be left alone! Just get the hell out of here or I'll shoot you!"

Ken flicked his eyes toward Nicky.

Nicky saw it too.

He was going to shoot.

Nicky didn't have time to think.

She moved her finger on the trigger, and she fired.

The deafening sound of the gunshot filled the room.

Jerry gasped as he was hit in the shoulder, and his gun fell to the ground.

Ken was on top of Jerry in a heartbeat, pinning him to the ground. Nicky grabbed Jerry's whiskey bottle and flung it to the side. It smashed against the wall and shattered. Jerry yelled in pain, and he struggled against Ken.

"Where are they?" Ken shouted at Jerry. "Where the hell are they?"

Jerry was trying to throw Ken off, but Ken was having none of it. Jerry kicked at Ken, but Ken blocked each kick. He wasn't about to let Jerry go.

"Where are the girls?" he demanded.

"Get the hell off me!" Jerry yelled. "I don't know what you're talking about!"

Nicky came over with her handcuffs out. While Ken had him pinned, Nicky twisted Ken's arms behind his back and handcuffed him.

He'd almost won—but they had him. And now, the truth would come out.

***

The interrogation room was cold with the weight of the unanswered questions in the air. Nicky took her seat across from Jerry, Ken beside her. Jerry refused to look at them, his hands cuffed behind his back. He was a balding man with prison tattoos, and when Nicky looked at him, all she saw was his future: he'd be back in a cell before he knew it. Threatening to kill two agents while still on probation was a bad look. Plus, the weapon he'd used had been illegally obtained.

It was all going to end poorly for Jerry Bocanegra. But one question remained: was he the kidnapper?

Did he have Susie and Sammy Miller?

Nicky cleared her throat, staring Jerry down as she shuffled his file in front of her. "Quite the long history you have with the law, Mr. Bocanegra," she said. "Do you see where this is headed?"

Jerry didn't answer.

"This is going to go poorly for you," she said. "And I'll be honest, I don't give a damn about you. I just want to know one thing: where are the girls?"

Jerry still didn't answer. Nicky sighed and opened up the file, taking out a photo of Susie and Sammy. She slid it across the table.

"Where are these girls, Jerry?"

He sneered, barely glancing at the photo. "Never seen them in my life."

"Just tell me where you've taken them," Nicky said. Her patience was running thin.

Jerry spat onto the floor, making Nicky's stomach curl with disgust. He was a vile man. He never should have been released from jail.

"You drive an ATV, don't you, Jerry?" Nicky said. "That's what you used when you kidnapped those girls all those years ago. Now you've done it again, haven't you?" Her eyes hardened, but still, Jerry refused to look at her. "You took Susie and Sammy Miller, Jerry. Where are they?"

Finally, his beady brown eyes met Nicky's. "I don't know who the hell those girls are. I haven't touched anyone since I got out of jail."

Nicky held up the file again. "We know all about your crimes, Jerry," she said. "And we know you did it again. So why don't you just—"

Jerry suddenly thrashed in the chair. "I didn't take anyone, damn it! You were on my property, I had every right to pull my gun on you!"

"You're about to be charged with abduction and maybe murder, Jerry," Nicky said, trying to keep her voice steady. "We can make the charges stick. You'll be spending the rest of your life in prison."

Jerry laughed. "That's the point, isn't it?"

Nicky glanced at Ken. This guy was unhinged, and he probably wasn't going to be much help. She needed to lean on someone who actually knew something.

"How can you say that?" Nicky said. "They're innocent girls. You took them. They're probably scared, and—"

"Let me ask you something." Jerry looked up at her, his eyes white and angry. "How long did you spend in jail? How long did you have to deal with those animals around you? You don't know what it's like. I didn't hurt any girls. I don't know those redhead chicks at all. Never seen 'em. And you know what? They're not even my type."

Nicky was disgusted. And she wasn't buying this. Jerry was a violent, unhinged creep, and he deserved to be behind bars.

"Let's just cut the shit, Jerry," Nicky said. "Where were you on the night of August third?"

Jerry laughed. "Where was I? I was nowhere near here, I can tell ya that much."

"And it's your idea of a good time to kidnap girls and—"

"I didn't kidnap anyone!" Jerry shouted. "I didn't touch those girls. And you can't keep me locked up for something I didn't do!"

Nicky drummed her fingers on the table, feeling frustration build up inside of her. They weren't getting anywhere.

"Mr. Bocanegra, you are on probation for the rest of your life," she said. "We can keep you here and we can charge you with whatever we like. You'll never get out. So why don't you just tell us where you've taken those girls."

Jerry tapped his feet on the ground. "And what if I don't?"

"Then this will be a lot harder on you," Ken said.

"Were you with Sammy and Susie Miller, Jerry?" Nicky snapped. "What did you do with those girls?"

"I don't know who they are," Jerry said. "I don't know them. I don't know anything. I didn't touch anybody, I haven't kidnapped anybody."

Nicky waved the photo in the air. "Then tell us where they are!"

"I told you I don't know!" Jerry yelled.

A knock on the door interrupted the interrogation. A flustered-looking cop rushed in, his face red and his hair frazzled. "Agent Lyons, Agent Walker—you need to come out here now."

Nicky exchanged a look with Ken. "We're a little busy right now," Nicky said. "Can it wait?"

He shook his head. "No. It's important."

She shot Jerry a look, and he wore a smug expression. "Better go tend to your flowers," he said.

Nicky ignored him, not giving him the satisfaction of knowing he'd pissed her off. She and Ken stood up and followed the officer out of the interrogation room, into the office.

"This better be important," Nicky began, but she was cut off.

The officer looked at her with panicked eyes. "There's someone on the phone…" He took a breath. "They're saying they know who the kidnapper is—and they'll only talk to you."

CHAPTER SIXTEEN

A smooth, sultry female voice came in on the other end of his phone. He had asked to speak to the agent in charge of the investigation—but he hadn't known the fed he'd be talking to would sound so attractive. A smile curled at his lips as he listened to her words.

"Who is this?" she asked.

He had her attention. An image began to form of the beautiful woman behind the phone. He hadn't expected to be so intrigued by the person in charge of the investigation against him. This was an interesting turn of events, and it would make it all the more fun.

"Hello there," he said into the phone. "You're the agent in charge?"

"I'm Agent Nicky Lyons of the FBI, yes," she said. "I'm told you know who took Susie and Sammy Miller."

Nicky Lyons? That name sounded so familiar… where had he heard it before?

He looked over his shoulder, into the dark room, where he had not one set of twins—but two.

All four of his beautiful twins were there: Susie, Sammy, London, and Paris.

All of them were tied up and gagged. All of them were struggling.

And they were all his.

"I'm not sure," he said, keeping his eyes on the girls. He leaned back in his chair and popped a grape in his mouth, enjoying the moment he'd been waiting so long for. "What makes you think I know anything about their kidnapping?"

"What kind of sick game is this?" Nicky said. "I know you do. And I need you to tell me where you are, so we can get the girls back."

"I'm sure the girls would rather be here," he said, his voice cold. "With me."

There was a pause on the other end. He pictured Nicky processing his words; processing that he was serious.

"Listen, asshole," she said. "I don't have time for your games. If you know anything about the girls, then you need to tell me now."

"But maybe I don't want to tell you," he said. "Maybe I just want to sit here and watch them."

He could see her in his mind's eye, her face twisted in a mask of rage. But she was pretty when she was angry.

"You have them," Nicky said breathily.

He laughed and leaned back further in his chair, popping another grape in his mouth. He crunched down, and it made a loud SNAP as it popped between his teeth. "I have them, Agent Lyons."

"Where are you?" Her voice was shaking now.

"Where am I?" he said. "Oh, where I am you can never find me. But I'll tell you something: I have the girls in my special room. I like to play with them. I like to make them scream. They scream prettily, don't you think?"

A pause. "I need you to tell me where you are, so we can get them back."

"I'm not so sure the girls want to come back," he said.

He could hear her breathing on the other end of the line, harsh and ragged.

"You let them go," Nicky said. "If you let them go, we can talk about a deal."

"But if I let them go, I won't have anything to play with, will I?" he said. "They'll just leave, and I'd be all alone…"

He could practically hear her teeth grinding. "Who are you?"

He could tell she was truly afraid. What a shame. She should be afraid. She should tremble with fear in his presence.

"You're just dying to know, aren't you, Agent Lyons?" he taunted. "How about this… I can make you a deal. You can choose what happens to one of these beautiful girls. Listen carefully, Agent Lyons…"

A shaky breath on the other end of the line told him she was still there. Good. He smiled, looking into the terrified eyes of his four beautiful girls.

"I can let one of them go, Agent Lyons," he said. "One from either set of twins. Which one should I release?" He snickered. "But… there's a catch. It wouldn't be a game otherwise, would it?"

On the phone, Nicky said nothing, so he continued.

"I can let one twin go… but the other twin will die."

He bit into another grape. "I'll let you choose. One of these girls will live, and one of them will die. Which one do you want to live?"

On the phone, he heard her sharp intake of breath. He could imagine the look on her face, the way she'd be trembling as she listened to him.

"No," she whispered.

"Yes," he said. "Which one?"

He smiled. This was getting too good.

"Or," he said, "I can offer you an alternate choice. Both twins can stay with me. Alive. But they'll be my playthings—they'll never know freedom again."

No response came, but his smile only widened.

"Your choice, Agent Lyons. Will they both lose their freedom? Or will one die so the other can be free? Your choice."

CHAPTER SEVENTEEN

Nicky couldn't believe the horrible ultimatum she was listening to. The voice that came through the other end was distorted with some sort voice scrambler, and the techs were working quickly to try to trace the call—but nothing was coming in.

In the small police room, Nicky was surrounded by Ken and other officers who were listening in. She needed to negotiate, to get this bastard to not hurt any of the girls.

If they really were alive.

"How do I know you're telling the truth?" Nicky said into the phone. "How do I know you actually have them?"

"You don't," the voice said. "But if you want one of them to live, you're going to have to choose. Choose wisely."

Nicky stared at the floor. She was freaking out, and she knew it. She had to hold it together, to get everyone out of this room, to get somewhere she could think.

For a moment, she wondered if she should even believe this guy, who was clearly unstable.

"I don't understand why you're doing this," she said. "What's the point of all this? What are you getting out of it, personally?"

"Oh, but this is personal, Agent Lyons," the voice said, amused. "This is very, very personal."

She had to figure out this guy, find out what he wanted. Maybe there was a way to get him to give up whatever he wanted. Maybe there was a way of getting him to release the girls.

"Come on," she said. "You want to be famous, right? Some sort of mastermind criminal? Just tell me what you want."

The voice laughed. "You really don't get it, do you, Agent Lyons?"

"Get what?" she said. "I don't get what you want. Why are you doing this?"

The voice took a breath. "What I want, Agent Lyons, is a family."

Nicky's eyes widened. "Family? What are you talking about?"

"I want a family," he said. "And these two sets of twins—these beautiful, innocent girls—these are my family. I love them. I want them with me."

"You want a family? A family of what?" Nicky said, her voice shaking. "Those girls aren't your family, they're your victims. Let them go."

"I don't care what you call it," the voice said. "I just want a family to love. This is… just a family of my own invention. My own family."

Nicky shook her head. This guy was insane. But in a way, she was getting some of his pathology. It could be useful later, but she needed more out of him. She looked at the officer on the computer, who was trying to trace the call, but he just shook his head. Still no luck.

This guy was a ghost.

Time for another topic, one that would hopefully throw him off: "What about the vehicle you used to take the girls?" Nicky asked. "It was an ATV, correct?"

A pause on the other end told her what she needed to know. She'd been right about the ATV.

She thought back to what Yancy had said; how he'd met a guy in a bar, a guy who liked twins… a guy who said Rosie's name. It was a long shot, but Nicky decided to throw it out there. She shared a look with Ken first; he'd probably think she was crazy for this, but she had to do it.

"And does the name Rosie mean anything to you?"

"Rosie…"

Suddenly, there was an ear-grating snicker on the other end, and Nicky's head spun.

"You said your name was Nicky Lyons," the voice said. "My, that's where I've heard it before. The Lyons sisters…"

Nicky's world spun. No. This couldn't be him. The man who'd taken her all those years ago. It couldn't be.

Then he said, "I know the tale. I'm sorry, Agent Lyons, but that wasn't my work. I wouldn't have let you get away without killing the other. I'm sorry you were so weak, though—my girls here are strong. They won't abandon their sisters."

Nicky was shaking, all the way to her core. "What do you mean without killing the other? Is Rosie alive?"

Across the room, Ken shot Nicky a perplexed look—a look that told her to stop. This was about Sammy, Susie, London, and Paris. Not

Nicky and Rosie. She knew that, but this was the closest she'd been in years to getting a glimpse of the truth.

"I wouldn't know," the voice said. "That wasn't my work."

"But you know who did it."

He laughed again. "You are selfish, Agent Lyons, and you are weak. Now choose: which girl will I release?"

Nicky ground her teeth. "Where will you release her?"

"A location. I can't tell you, not yet."

Damn it. She needed more. She needed to think fast. "How would I get there? Would I need an ATV like you? Would a sedan work?"

He sniggered. "What a silly question; any will work."

So it wasn't that treacherous of a location, if Nicky could get there by car.

But would she be able to, or would he kill the girl before she could make the drop-off?

She stared at the floor, and then a thought struck her. "What if neither of us choose?"

"That is not an option. You will choose. Look at the twins, Agent Lyons," he said. "They must be so hungry. You can hear them, can't you?"

Nicky gasped. Yes, now she could hear the girls. They were crying, pleading with her to let them go. It was heartbreaking, but she couldn't give in to her emotions. She had to think.

She dug her fingernails into her palms. "What if I told you I was coming alone? No police, no one else—would you release one of them and let the other live?"

His laugh dug under her skin. "That wasn't part of the deal, Agent Lyons. Choose. Or I'll choose for you."

The techs turned up the volume on Nicky's phone, and the sounds of the girls filled the room. Scared girls, who were probably crying, who were probably so frightened. Nicky couldn't even begin to imagine what they were going through.

She couldn't afford to let her emotions overtake her.

She swallowed hard.

She realized she was shaking again. She was terrified. She couldn't do this.

"Agent Lyons?"

She had to choose. She had to.

"Agent Lyons?!"

79

No. She couldn't do this.

She couldn't say which one would live and which one would die.

"Keep them both," Nicky finally said. "Keep them both, and keep them alive."

The whole room seemed to sigh in relief.

"Very well," said the voice. "A strong choice, Agent Lyons. Maybe you've changed."

Nicky shook her head. "I'm not changing. I'm just keeping the best possible outcome for both of them."

"Oh, but you have changed," the voice said. "You've chosen life, not death. That's change, isn't it? I think it is."

Nicky closed her eyes. She couldn't bear it. She couldn't listen to what he had to say next. She knew what he was going to say.

"Agent Lyons?"

"Yes?" she said.

"I'll be in touch soon. The girls live—for now. In twenty-four hours, I might change my mind."

"Wait—what do you mean!?" Nicky exclaimed, panicked.

The voice laughed one last time. Then the line went dead.

Silence filled the room, and every officer looked pale-faced. They were all looking at Nicky, Ken included. She felt the weight of the world on her shoulders. Did she make the right choice? What was everyone thinking?

She had to break the silence; it was unbearable. She turned to the tech at the computer. "You really didn't trace anything?"

"Not a thing," the tech said. "I'm sorry."

Nicky looked at Ken, and she couldn't tell why—but he looked disappointed. Disappointed in her.

"Everyone," Nicky said, looking at the officers, "please allow Agent Walker and me the room."

After a moment, they all filed out, leaving her alone with Ken.

The room fell into silence again. Ken was sitting in a chair, running his hands through his black hair. Nicky didn't know what he was thinking, but it heightened her anxiety.

"Walker," she said, and he looked up, tired. "What are you thinking?"

Slowly, Ken stood up, running his hand over the back of his neck. "I'm thinking that I was worried about this with you being the leader of the team, Lyons. Your personal investment in this case."

She swallowed, looking away. "Because I brought up Rosie."

"It wasn't the time."

"Wasn't it?" Nicky shot back. "He knows her, Ken. I had to make sure it wasn't the same guy who took me."

"Do you think it is?"

"No. The way he talks is different. But I think he knows him." She rubbed her face. "I had to pursue it. I had to know."

Ken said nothing, watching her.

Finally, Nicky looked up at him. "I'm not apologizing. If I'm the leader of this team, then I have to pursue every lead. You would have tried the same thing."

"I would not have," he said. "I would have stayed on track with the case, and nothing else."

Nicky was growing angrier by the second. "I'd expect you to be on my side about this. We're partners, Agent Walker. No—not just partners. I'm the leader of the team. Which means I make the calls, not you."

He shrugged, looking away. "You're right. But don't think I won't let the chief know that you're getting too personal about a case that involves you, when we've got four missing girls on our hands here that need to be saved. Who knows what that psychopath has planned for twenty-four hours from now?"

Shaking, Nicky turned away. She knew there was truth to what Ken was saying, but her pride made it so she wouldn't back down. She'd made the right call in the end. The twins would stay alive. Asking about Rosie hadn't distracted from that.

But she also felt the room crushing in around her. Because if she didn't find this guy and save those girls, it would all be on her. As irritated as she was with Ken, she needed him with her on this. And she was still the leader.

So she said, "Come on, Agent Walker. We have more work to do."

CHAPTER EIGHTEEN

Back at the motel room, Nicky pulled her laptop close and stared at the screen. She had to find him—she had no intention of going to sleep tonight. She had to prove she was the right person to lead this task force and catch this monster before he found another victim. The online database was open, a drop-down menu pulled up with all active warrants, her fingers tapping out a rhythm on the keyboard as she typed in each name. There had to be a connection out there, one she wasn't seeing.

Across from her, Ken was working away as well, but they hadn't talked since they got back in. Nicky knew he wasn't impressed with how she'd handled the phone call. And in truth, the case at hand likely did have nothing to do with what happened to Rosie. But still—if there was even a hope this kidnapper knew who took Rosie, then Nicky had to keep that in mind.

Until then, she needed to find him.

Searching for warrants had brought her no leads, so she decided to look back into the evidence from both crime scenes when each set of twins went missing.

She went back to the beginning and read through the notes, the pictures, the interviews.

As she went through the photos, it was hard not to remember how terrified she'd been when she'd been talking with that monster. She shivered and felt sick. He was twisted and deranged, and Nicky had no proof he'd keep the girls alive; only his word. But sometimes psychopaths abided by their own rules, so Nicky was banking that he'd keep all four twins alive for at least twenty-four hours.

As far as forensic evidence left at each crime scene, there wasn't much. Both events had been followed by a storm the next day, and Nicky noted that the kidnapper had probably planned that and checked the weather before hatching his plan. There were a few strands of hair at each scene, though, belonging to the victims. Nothing that pointed to who the kidnapper was.

No prints either.

She gave up on the photos and moved on to transcripts of interviews. There was a lot of dead space, but she got the sense the detectives had felt they had nothing to go on, and they'd stuck to the basics. She saw the questions they'd asked the survivors, and it was clear they'd wanted to get names, family members, anyone who'd been close to the victims.

But this kidnapper was far more organized. He was smart and careful. He had left no evidence behind, made sure it would all get naturally washed away. Nicky felt sick.

This was going nowhere. But there was one more detail about the crimes that she hadn't focused enough on—and those were the tchotchke dolls that were left behind at each scene.

She went back to her notes and read through the details. It was clear that he'd wanted to leave behind something, even though it was a clue to his identity.

"What are you doing, Lyons?" Ken asked.

Nicky looked at him over her laptop screen and tried not to think about how she'd let him down earlier. "I'm looking back into the dolls," she said. "Maybe we can get a serial number and find out where they came from. That could narrow down his general location."

"That sounds reasonable," Ken said, looking back at his screen. "I was reading through transcripts of interviews, but I've got nothing."

"Yeah," Nicky said. "Let me call Grace and get some intel on these dolls."

It was an excuse to get away from the screen, to not think about the fact she was coming up with nothing. She couldn't think about those girls, pinned down and crying for help, because she didn't think she could go on like that. If she let herself feel what those girls were feeling and what they were going to have to go through, she didn't think she'd be able to go on, either.

She dialed Grace's number as she walked outside, the cool night air filling her lungs as she breathed in deeply. It was easy enough to get Grace on the phone; she was on the late shift and already had her report done for the day.

Grace answered on the second ring. "Agent Lyons," she said through a yawn. "How's it going?"

"Still trying to find a connection in that evidence."

"You'll find it," Grace said. "You guys are good."

"Thanks for the vote of confidence. Listen, I have a question about the tchotchkes that the unsub left behind. Do you know if any of them have the same serial number?"

"Let me check evidence…" Nicky heard clacking on the other end of the line. "Yep, serial numbers on both sets. The dolls were sold together."

"Twins," Nicky said. That wasn't a coincidence. "Can you tell me where they were purchased?" she asked.

"I'm looking into them now. They're very rare, old dolls, not even made anymore. Only two shops in the whole state carry them."

Nicky's heart picked up. "What are the names of the shops?"

"One's called Cynthia's Dolls, owned by a Cynthia Jones. The other is named Dolls 'R' Us, owned by a Jason Smith. You think they'll remember the guy?"

Nicky's mind was whirling again. "Maybe," she said. "I'll get back to you on that. Right now, I need you to look up the addresses for both businesses."

"I can send them to your phone. Jason's shop is close, an hour from you, but hold on, I'm just on their website right now and…" Grace paused. "It looks like they don't even carry those dolls anymore, and haven't in over five years. According to the serial numbers on the dolls at our crime scenes, they're newer models—made at least in the last two years."

Nicky paused, taking this all in. "So it had to come from Cynthia's."

"That's right. And you might not like this one, but it's four hours away."

"That's fine." Nicky was already walking back into the motel room. "I need you to dig up all the information you can find on this Cynthia Jones."

"You got it."

"Thanks, Grace." Nicky hung up and faced Ken, who was reading something on his screen. "I found our connection," she said.

"What?" Ken said, looking up from his screen.

"The tchotchkes were sold together in two sets, but this store called Cynthia's is the only place that sells that set. If we can find out who bought them, then—"

"We'll have a might tighter list of suspects," Ken said.

"Exactly. Only issue is that it's four hours away, so we should get going so we can be there by opening."

"You wanna pull an all-nighter?" Ken asked. "Lyons, no offense, but you look pretty tired. Maybe you'll let me drive for once so you can get some shut-eye."

Nicky hesitated. She was exhausted, but she hated relinquishing control of the wheel. "I don't know, Walker."

"Just for the way there. You can drive us back."

It felt like a compromise she could live with. "Okay," she said. "But we need to go now."

CHAPTER NINETEEN

Nicky settled into the passenger seat of her car, realizing that she'd never actually sat in it before. It felt weird to let Ken adjust her seat and her mirrors, and Nicky regretted agreeing to let him take the wheel. But it was too late now, and they were backing out of the motel lot, the headlights slicing the darkness.

Nicky still hadn't slept, but she was wired and ready. If she knew anything about this unsub, it was that he'd probably left his hometown a long time ago. Still, she couldn't shake the feeling that she was close to finding him. It was like he was tugging at the hem of her shirt, and if she could just go after him, she'd find him. She just knew it—and she'd be damned if she wasn't going to take that feeling with her.

The road felt long. Even though Nicky's mind was racing, her body was undeniably tired. Her eyes burned and ached, and all she wanted to do was close them and sleep for a few hours. That wasn't an option. Instead, she found a classic rock station on the radio and listened to that, trying to keep herself mentally sharp.

The last thing she wanted to do was nod off and lose control. At least if she was awake, she could be aware of everything happening around her. It wasn't necessarily that she distrusted Ken behind the wheel, but she just… hated this feeling of being a passenger. It brought back too much.

She tried to fight it, tried to keep herself alert, but she felt her eyes drooping. She was definitely going to have to stop and get some caffeine somewhere along the way, but until then…

Suddenly, Nicky could feel the car jolt forward and slow down, just like a dream. She opened her eyes and couldn't see anything outside the window. The sky was black. She looked up at the dashboard and saw that it was three a.m. They weren't moving.

She had slept through the trip. She turned to Ken, who was sleeping. What the…? Did Ken fall asleep behind the wheel?

Nicky yawned, trying to keep herself awake, but she felt airy and dreamy. She needed to stay focused, to find out where the tchotchkes had been bought.

"Walker, wake up." Nicky nudged him.

But then his head rolled to the side, and Nicky's heart leapt into her throat.

He had no eyes.

His throat was slit.

There was blood everywhere.

He was dead.

Nicky screamed. She got out of the car, only to find herself alone in a forest. Not a Florida forest—a West Virginia forest.

This was the same night she'd escaped the kidnapper. She was back.

A voice rang in her mind: "I'm sorry you were so weak, though—my girls here are strong. They won't abandon their sisters."

"I'm not weak!" Nicky screamed at the pitch-black sky. "I was going to get help! I went back!"

Suddenly, a pair of giant red eyes appeared in the sky. "You were weak. You left her to die."

"No!" Nicky screamed. "No! I'm stronger than that! I'm stronger than you! I went back! I got help!"

"Help came too late."

A deafening screech rang out, a screech that Nicky knew too well.

Suddenly, she was falling.

Next thing she knew, she was back in the car.

No—not the car. She was staring at the ceiling of the hotel room.

She had awoken screaming.

Nicky's heart was pounding, and she looked down at her hands. They were covered in blood. It was dripping from her elbows onto the floor.

Her heart stopped.

She waited for the feeling to pass. It didn't. Instead, her heart started racing even faster, the blood pounding in her ears.

She couldn't move.

She couldn't breathe.

She felt like she was choking on her own heartbeat.

Dreaming, she told herself. I'm still dreaming.

Wake up!

Lyons, wake up!

No, no, no. No, no, no, no, no.

"You're going to die alone."

Nicky's eyes snapped open. She was in her car, someplace on the highway. She knew this landscape. She was in Florida.

"No… no…" Her body was shaking.

It was just a dream, that's all. It was just a damn dream.

"Lyons." Ken's brusque voice cut into her mind, and her eyes snapped to him. Part of her feared she'd see the same imagery she saw in her dream—of Ken dead. But he was alive, and he was blinking at her.

"You good?" he asked her. "You were making noise in your sleep…"

Nicky felt herself shiver. She looked around the empty highway they were speeding down and felt a loss of control that made her head spin.

"I'm fine, just… can I drive?" Nicky asked.

"You sure you're okay to drive?" Ken asked. "You looked like you were having a nightmare or something."

"Yeah, I'm fine." Nicky kept her head down as she took the wheel.

"You sure?"

"Yeah, I'm good."

Ken didn't seem convinced, but he slapped on the blinker and pulled over. Nicky got out of the car, unnerved by the cool breeze in the air, then traded spots with Ken.

Nicky kept driving at the same speed, but now she was behind the wheel. Slowly, she worked on slowing her heart rate, on calming the panic that was threatening to overtake her. She felt the highway wind under her tires, the black sky above her head. She was safe. She was fine. This was just a dream. She held onto the wheel, feeling her hands start to shake as her body started to calm down. She was still on high alert, and she knew she'd have to be extra vigilant until she was sure that she had returned to reality. But no matter what else happened, she felt confident that she wouldn't be dreaming again tonight—not after that.

After several minutes of quietly driving through the night, Ken asked, "You gonna tell me what that was about?"

"I was just dreaming," Nicky replied.

"Right," Ken said, not buying it. "About what?"

"Nothing… personal, I guess."

"Nicky, you don't sweat like that for nothing."

Nicky felt herself tighten up, but she didn't say a word. She glanced at Ken, who was sitting in the passenger seat with his hands folded in his lap. He was looking straight ahead—at the road—like he was trying to keep his eyes open.

"I know you been through a lot," Ken said. "I can imagine what it was about."

Nicky took a breath. She wouldn't tell him all the details of the dream. Seeing him dead—that was something she could keep to herself. "My sister," she said. "But it was… different. I had the voice in my head, the voice of the kidnapper from when he called us. I was thinking about what he said… how I'm weak for leaving Rosie behind."

"You were a scared kid," Ken said. "You went to get help. If you hadn't, who knows…" Ken stopped himself, likely knowing that if he kept going, he'd strike a chord. But it was too late; Nicky knew what he was thinking, and it was the truth.

If Nicky hadn't left that night, she'd have met the same fate as Rosie. At best, Rosie was alive somewhere, being held hostage and tortured for years. At worst, she was dead in a ditch somewhere.

But Rosie wasn't the only one. There were so many girls out there, being held captive, being hurt. And Nicky, of all people, had the power to save them. She had the power to make sure that none of that would happen again.

That was why she had become an FBI agent.

That was why she couldn't let herself fail.

"I know you're strong," Ken said, breaking the silence. "You'll get through this."

Nicky felt her heart clench, and she knew it wasn't all about the dream. She knew it wasn't about the past.

It was about the future.

It was about the girls she hadn't saved.

It was about the girls she might be able to save if she just did her job.

"Thanks, Walker," Nicky said.

He cleared his throat. "For the record, I get why you wanted to ask that creep on the phone about your sister. And if he does know her, that's pretty remarkable, but he could just be messing with you, like we thought Yancy was messing with you."

Nicky swallowed, her throat tight. She hadn't considered that, too blinded by how familiar this all was. "You could be right," she said. "I won't let it distract from the case again. This is about Susie, Sammy, London, and Paris. We'll find them."

They continued through the night in a comfortable silence. The moon was out, the sky a midnight blue. Nicky stared out at the highway, feeling her pulse slow as her mind started to clear.

But memories of Rosie threatened to come back. She remembered one time, when she was nine and Rosie was eight, Rosie had been getting picked on at school. A couple of girls had been teasing her, and Rosie—who was never the type to tell an adult—had been having a hard time.

One afternoon, when Nicky came home from school, Rosie was just as frazzled as she'd been when she walked out the door.

"Rosie," Nicky said, rushing to her sister's side. "What happened?"

"Nothing," Rosie said, but she was trembling.

"Nothing?" Nicky was incredulous. "You're shaking."

"It's nothing," Rosie repeated. "I'm okay."

"No, it's not nothing," Nicky said, taking her sister by the shoulders. "Tell me what happened."

"It was nothing," Rosie said. "Just a couple of girls were being mean—"

"What did they say?" Nicky asked, fuming with anger.

"Nothing. It's okay."

"No, it's not okay," Nicky said. "What did they say?"

"They were just saying stuff about me," Rosie said, keeping her eyes trained on the ground.

"What did they say?" Nicky asked.

Rosie didn't respond, shaking her head.

"Tell me," Nicky said.

"No." Rosie's voice was low. "I want to forget about it."

"I can't forget about it," Nicky said. "They're being mean to you."

"It's okay," Rosie said softly, looking up at her sister. "I can take it."

Nicky felt her stomach turn over. "How can you take it? They're picking on you! I can't believe you let them! I'm your big sister, Rosie—you have to let me protect you sometimes."

"I don't need protecting," Rosie said, and she walked away, heading for their room.

"What are you talking about?" Nicky asked, running after her into their shared room. "They're picking on you! Why are you letting them?"

"I don't need you to protect me," Rosie said, her voice shaking now. "I can fend for myself. I can stand up for myself."

They were at a weird phase in their relationship, where Rosie was getting older and wanting more independence from Nicky.

"I'm always going to protect you," Nicky said. "You're my sister."

"You can't protect me from everything," Rosie said. "I don't need you to."

"Yes, you do," Nicky said. "You need me to protect you from everything. I'm your sister—it's my job."

Nicky's heart pulled as she ripped herself from the memory. Nicky would've done anything to protect Rosie back then. But when they were teenagers, it was Nicky who'd escaped the kidnapper.

Anxiety tore through her. She'd been through this before—she'd been having these thoughts for years, and had gone over them with her psychiatrist countless times. He said it was called survivor's guilt. But sometimes, Nicky felt like she really did deserve the anxiety for leaving Rosie behind.

After what felt like forever, Nicky and Ken arrived in Rockwood. It was a tiny town, but there was no crime in the quaint village, so Nicky and Ken didn't have anything to go by. They drove down the main street, looking at the window displays in the empty stores and going past the dark buildings until they reached the edge of town, which was surrounded by the forest. There was nothing. Especially in the dead of night, not a soul lingered in this town.

They found Cynthia's doll shop on the outskirts of town, but naturally, it was too early for it to be open.

"What should we do?" Ken asked. "We've got a couple hours till sunlight."

Nicky pulled the car into the parking lot in front of Cynthia's and parked the car in an empty spot. They could wait it out here until sunrise. "You might as well get a couple hours of sleep, Walker," Nicky said. "Don't stay up on my account."

"You're not gonna try to sleep more?" he asked.

"After that nightmare, I think I'll pass."

"Lucky me," Ken muttered as he leaned back in the seat and closed his eyes.

Nicky was still on edge as Ken fell asleep. She glanced at him once his eyes were closed, trying not to think about the horrific image of him she'd seen in her nightmare.

Leaning back in her own seat, Nicky shut her eyes. Soon, she'd have the answers she was looking for.

Soon, she'd save those twins. She wouldn't leave them behind. Not like she'd left Rosie.

CHAPTER TWENTY

Nicky opened her eyes to a loud knock on glass. Sunlight pierced her eyes, and startled, she looked to her left—only to see a large woman scowling at her through the window.

"Walker, wake up," Nicky said, and Ken's eyes popped open beside her. Nicky rolled down the window, letting in the warm morning air. She must have fallen asleep.

The scowling woman was heavyset and wore a long purple dress, adorned with gold necklaces. Strands of gray hair fell into her face, but she brushed them away with the back of her hand. She was older, and had graying hair in a sort of mullet. Her brow was creased into a deep frown that made her deep-set eyes seem unhappy.

"What in God's name are you doing in my parking lot?" she asked.

"Your parking lot?" Nicky asked, still half-delirious. "We're with the FBI."

"FBI? The hell are you doin' here?"

"Are you Cynthia?" Nicky asked. "You own the doll store?"

"Yeah, that's me… what's it to the FBI?"

"We were hoping we could come in and talk to you. Would that be okay?"

The woman's frown deepened, and she glanced to the store behind her. "I'm not a fan of cops."

"We're not cops," Nicky said. "We're FBI agents. We're just here to talk."

The woman didn't seem convinced. "You mind showing me some ID?" she asked.

Nicky and Ken exchanged a glance. This woman was clearly suspicious of them, but they had to find out what they could—right now, there was nothing else to go on, and they couldn't figure out a way to get Cynthia alone without appearing suspicious. With a sigh, Nicky grabbed her wallet and handed her FBI identification to the woman.

The woman studied the badge for several long seconds, and then handed it back to Nicky.

"All this over my doll store?" Cynthia asked. "It's been breakin' my heart these days, but I ain't done nothin' to make the FBI pay me a visit."

"Could we talk in your shop?" Nicky asked.

Cynthia looked flabbergasted as she mulled it over, but finally, she stepped away from the window. "All right then. Come on in."

Nicky and Ken climbed out of the car, Nicky rubbing her eyes as Ken stretched his arms.

Cynthia unlocked the door and then jerked her thumb for them to follow her inside. She was clearly irritated, and Nicky wondered if it was just her personality. She seemed awfully crotchety for someone who dealt with wares mostly for children.

The three of them walked into the store, and Nicky was surprised to see how large it was. It didn't look like much from the outside, but the inside was big, with a high ceiling, glass cases that filled the middle of the store, and a checkout counter to the right.

There was a lot of merchandise. On the shelves, there were toys of all kinds in addition to dolls: action figures, stuffed animals, and even action figures of stuffed animals. There was a wall of board games, and another wall of stationery and art supplies.

"How long have you owned this shop?" Nicky asked.

"Thirteen years," Cynthia said. She took her spot on the other side of the sales counter while Nicky and Ken remained on the other side.

"Do you keep records of sales here?" Nicky asked. "As in, records of who buys what?"

She wheezed out a laugh. "Of course not. People buy things as they please."

"What about security footage?" Nicky asked.

"Honey, I'm not breaking the bank around here," Cynthia said, hand on her wide hip. "No cameras. Just toys. Wanna buy some?"

"No thank you," Nicky said. "Actually, I'm hoping to inquire about specific dolls I understand you might sell here." Nicky took out her phone, bringing up the photos of the tchotchke dolls found at each crime scene.

Cynthia leaned in, brows pinched, and observed the photo. "Yeah, I got those. It's not a big seller, but I have about three or four of them on the shelf. Sell them in pairs, usually."

Nicky's heart raced. "Do you remember who purchased these dolls, Cynthia? It's very important." Nicky wondered if she would describe the same man Yancy claimed he saw at the bar.

"Oh, I remember him, all right," she said. "Name's Nial Prat, and everyone knows him real well around here."

"What does he look like?"

"Fat, bald, you know, real ugly fella. Real troublemaker too, might I add."

"Does he have a dagger tattoo?" Nicky asked, her heart beating louder. Yancy had said the guy in the bar—the guy who mentioned Rosie—had one.

Cynthia shrugged. "I don't know. Nial's a weird guy—has a lot of tattoos, anyway. I'm too busy runnin' this place to worry about the people who buy my merchandise."

"Have you seen this man in the past couple of days?"

"Nial? Yeah, he's here sometimes, hangs out at the bar."

"The bar across town?" Ken asked.

"Yeah. He's a regular. Picks up orders every now and then."

"Can you describe what he was wearing? What he looks like?"

"Well.." She frowned, thinking. "Black T-shirt, I think. Oh, shit, I don't remember what color it was. Jeans, I think. Black jeans. You can find him at the trailer park on the east side of town—he's always there, from what I know. We're a small town. Everyone more or less knows each other. Not sure which trailer is his, though; I've never been invited over."

Nicky nodded. She came from a small town that was surrounded by mountains and beautiful scenery, where everyone knew everyone and everyone knew everyone's business. Nelly, West Virginia, was a long way from here. The crisp mountain air carried the scents of pine trees and flowers and was heavy with moisture. It wasn't like the warm, sunny atmosphere of Florida, not at all.

But she remembered that there were a few bad apples back then, too, and everyone would know the stories. She wondered if Cynthia could shed some more light on who Nial Prat really was.

"Can you tell us anything else about him?" Nicky asked. "Anything that might be relevant?"

"Well, he's been in trouble with the law more than once, that's for sure," Cynthia said. "Seems like every time he drinks a little too much, he's getting arrested for something."

95

"What does he drink?" Ken asked.

"Whiskey," she said. "Always whiskey. He's a mean drunk. Has a big mouth. Whatever he says, he always tries to act like he's a big shot."

"Is he married?" Nicky asked.

"Nial? Oh, he was married once—about a hundred years ago," Cynthia said, shaking her head. "But sadly, his wife passed away. They had a daughter, but she's all grown up. Beautiful girl."

Nicky nodded. "This might be an odd question, but has Nial ever mentioned anything about twins?"

Cynthia's brows pinched. "Twins? I don't think so. He only has one kid."

Nicky wasn't sure what to make of all this. Just because Cynthia never heard him mention twins didn't mean he wasn't their guy, and the fact that he'd purchased the dolls—that was everything.

He had to be the right guy.

"When exactly did you last see him?" Ken asked.

"I don't know." Cynthia thought for a moment. "Couple days, no, probably a week ago. He comes in sometimes, gets a few things, and leaves. I doubt he's been in here these past few days. He's been s'posed to be workin', but I haven't seen him there either. Trust me, if he's anywhere, he's probably at the trailer park."

Nicky nodded. They had more than enough to go off. They were at least a few steps closer to catching the culprit. Now, they just needed to go to the trailer park and look for Nial Prat.

"Thank you, Cynthia," Nicky said. "We appreciate the help."

"Yeah. Be seeing you."

Ken and Nicky left the toy shop and stepped into the sunny day. They headed across the parking lot to their car. Nicky got in the driver's seat, as usual.

"You think this guy is the one?" Ken asked, strapping in his seat belt.

"I think so," Nicky said, staring out the window. "He has to be, if he's the one who purchased the dolls. We just need to find him and bring him in. He has to crack eventually."

Nicky looked around the town. It really was a nice place. She wondered how she could be further away from home, but she couldn't deny the fact that she was in a small, quaint town. And sometimes towns like this held the darkest secrets of all.

Nicky started the car and made her way toward the trailer park. She knew it was going to be a long day. There was a lot to do and a lot to figure out. She just hoped they could put the pieces of this puzzle together in time to catch the culprit—before the twenty-four hours were up.

He wouldn't win this time. Not on her watch.

CHAPTER TWENTY ONE

The trailer park was more spread out than Nicky had imagined it would be. The road split into two directions and Nicky and Ken turned right. They drove slowly down the main road, past the various trailers, a gray plastic lawn chair hanging from a nail in a tree trunk, and made a right. They drove slowly down the main road, and that was when the residents started to take notice of them. Their faces were hard and lined, marred by dirt and fatigue. The men wore ragged clothes, the two halves of their pants flapping against their thighs. Here and there a woman was attired in a long dress, the frills of which were torn at the hems. Children were ragged as well, their gappy smiles showing missing teeth. The trailers were dilapidated, little more than hovels erected from old boards and sheets of rusted tin.

"Not a friendly-looking bunch," Nicky muttered as she drove. She had a bad feeling about this.

They drove by a few trailers, some of which had broken windows, and others that looked like they'd seen better days. The kids came out to watch them, and some of the women left their houses to stand on their porches, watching with hard, dark eyes.

"We might want to go slowly around here," Ken said. "Something doesn't feel right."

"I know. I can't shake this feeling either."

They came around one final bend and saw the entire trailer park in its full glory, with about twenty trailers to choose from.

Just then, Nicky's phone, sitting in the center console of the car, started vibrating. She frowned; it was early, and the only person who ever called her was work.

"Check that, will you?" Nicky asked Ken as she drove, looking for a decent spot to park that wouldn't end with her car getting keyed.

Ken checked Nicky's phone. "It's Chief Franco."

"Put it on speaker."

Ken did as he was told, and moments later, the chief's gruff voice filled the car. "Agent Lyons, bad news."

Nicky's stomach felt sick. "What's going on, Chief?"

He took a deep breath. "You're not gonna like this. Two more girls have gone missing. Twins."

Nicky and Ken exchanged a look. "When?" Nicky asked.

"Just now. I just got the call. They were at home, about three hours from where the other two went missing, with their families, and now they're gone. The families are frantic. We need to move on this."

Nicky gripped the steering wheel. "Chief, have you been in contact with the families of the other victims?"

"Yes. Now that this has happened, I was in contact with all of them. They're all terrified."

"Do their descriptions match?" Nicky asked.

"They do, yes. And two dolls were left at the scene. I wanted to tell you myself, Lyons. This thing is picking up." He paused. "You need to find this guy."

"Yes, Chief," Nicky said, trying to keep her cool. "We're on it."

"I know you are," he said. "Just find him. Grace will send you the details on the new victims."

The call ended, and Nicky slowed the car down. She and Ken were silent. They didn't know what to say. Two more twins. Two more dolls. There was no way this day could get any worse, but if Nicky was lucky… then maybe this very park they were in would have the girls in it. Maybe they were already here.

But a seed of doubt grew in her. Nicky's life was rarely that generous.

Just then, her phone vibrated again. This time, Ken checked it himself. "It's the precinct we were at yesterday," Ken said.

"What?" Nicky scowled. "Chief said the new kidnappings happened far away, it'd be out of their jurisdiction. Maybe it's an update on Jerry Bocanegra. Answer and put it on speaker."

Ken did as he was told, and Nicky said, "Hello?" into the phone.

"Agent Lyons?" a shaky male voice said.

"That's me. What's going on?"

"You… you have another phone call."

All at once, Nicky's world stood still. Her teeth clenched.

Another phone call.

It had to be from him. The kidnapper. Here for more games, more ultimatums.

"Put him through," Nicky said. She pulled over at the side, outside of a trailer, and parked the car, no longer caring where she was or who saw her.

Moments later, the voice—still distorted by the voice scrambler—came through.

"Hello, Agent Lyons. It's me again."

Nicky's hands gripped the steering wheel so hard her knuckles were white. She made sure to keep her voice as even as possible. She couldn't let on how much this was getting to her. She couldn't let this person see that she was rattled.

"I know," Nicky said. "Who are you?"

"You don't need to know that," came the reply. "I have your little set of twins… three sets now. I told you within twenty-four hours, I might change my mind on the way things… worked out."

Nicky gritted her teeth. So this was what he meant.

"Everyone is still alive?" she asked.

"For now," said the voice.

Sitting in the passenger seat, Ken widened. His hand went to his gun. Nicky nodded.

"Where are you?" Nicky asked.

"Does it matter?" the voice said. "You have to listen to me. You have to be smart about this. You have to listen to my demands."

"Demands?" Nicky asked.

"Yes, Agent Lyons. Demands. If you do this, someone will live. I've been honest with you from the beginning. I've always been honest with you. You have to be honest with me."

Nicky's throat was so tight, she felt her head might burst. She swallowed hard. "What do you want?"

"I have six beautiful girls with me now: Susie and Sammy Miller, London and Paris Knight, and my newest, cutest additions: Emma and Ella Sorenson."

"Don't you dare hurt them," Nicky said, her hands shaking.

A laugh came through the phone. "Don't get all emotional on me now, Agent Lyons… this stirs up some old memories for you, doesn't it? Well, it's okay. I don't want to kill all these girls." He paused. "Only one of them must die."

"What are you talking about?" Nicky tried to keep her voice firm, but a girl's life was in her hands, damn it. She wanted to rip through this phone and put this bastard down herself. But she was powerless.

"I have six girls here, Agent Lyons," the voice said. "But I only want five. So, I'll cut you a little deal: you choose one girl of the lot who I will kill, and the others will live."

"You know I won't," Nicky said.

"Oh, but Agent Lyons, you have to," he said. "You have to choose one. Because if you don't, I will kill every single one of them."

Nicky heard girls whimpering in the background of the call.

And she could have sworn... one of them was crying, a faint sob that echoed. The voice continued.

"You have until tomorrow to make your choice, Agent Lyons. Twenty-four hours. Tomorrow morning, by ten a.m., I'll take one girl out, and the others will be free. But I will only give you one day to pick. It's your greatest decision: one girl must die. It's your greatest responsibility. Make sure you're ready."

Girls in the background were crying. "Shhh," the kidnapper said. "It's okay. Everything's okay. I'm right here."

"This isn't a choice," Nicky said. "There is no choice."

"Oh, but there is," he said. "I've been more than fair with you. I wasn't this polite with the other girls. Well, I didn't give them a choice to begin with..."

Nicky's heart almost stopped. She felt like she couldn't breathe.

"So," he said. "Think hard, Agent Lyons. I'll see you tomorrow."

The line went dead.

In the car, it was silent. Ken stared out the window, his hand on his gun, his jaw tight.

Nicky stared forward. "We're out of time."

Ken nodded, clenching his fists. It was the worst feeling Nicky could imagine.

She had to choose one of the girls to die.

She had less than twenty-four hours.

"We have to go," Nicky said. She put the car in gear and continued driving through the park. Nicky's hands were shaking, and she had to take a series of deep breaths to keep herself from passing out.

They had to find Nial Prat's trailer, and they had to do it now, before Nicky was forced to make a choice she could never live with.

CHAPTER TWENTY TWO

Nicky parked in a visitors' parking area and got out of the car, her heart in her throat. Every wasted second felt like another second closer to the biggest failure of her career.

She could not let a single one of those girls die. Not one. And she didn't care who she had to tear through to find them.

Ken zipped out after her. As they stepped into the trailer park, they noticed the unfriendly eyes on them. Everyone was giving them sideways glances, and Nicky noticed that they were being stopped by a group of men near one of the trailers. The men were dressed in leather and chains, scars covered their skin, and tattoos swarmed their bodies. They were big and muscular men, dangerous-looking men who were looking at Ken and Nicky with menace in their eyes.

Nicky didn't care how intimidating they wanted to act. She was here for answers. "Excuse me," she said, holding eye contact with one of the men. She pulled out her badge, and Ken did the same. "We're with the FBI. Have you seen Nial Prat anywhere?"

The man scowled, not budging an inch. "I ain't seen him, lady," he said. "I don't think any of us have."

"I'll ask again," Nicky said, holding the man's gaze. "Have you seen Nial Prat in the last week?"

"I told you, lady," the man said. "I ain't seen him."

"You sure about that?" Ken asked.

The man grinned. He had a long, braided red beard. "I'm sure I ain't seen him, man."

Nicky took a deep breath to keep her voice neutral. She said, "I'd appreciate it if you and all your friends take a step back. This is official FBI business."

The man laughed. "If you want us to take a step back, lady, you better show us some damn respect."

"I don't need to show you any respect," Nicky said, her ire rising.

The men stared at them for a moment, then broke their gaze and looked away.

The bearded man shrugged and walked away, strutting and showing his behind to the two FBI agents.

Furious, Nicky tried to calm herself. She would not give in to these guys. She had more important things to worry about. "Listen, pal," she called after him, and the man turned. "Just tell me— have you seen Nial Prat in the last day?"

"No," the man said. "I haven't seen him. And even if I did, I wouldn't tell you, lady. You think you can just come here and patronize us? You think you can come here and treat us like trash? You think you can just come here and take whatever you want?"

Nicky's fists clenched. She didn't know why they were making her life so difficult, but she was going to find Prat, one way or another.

"Get out of here," the man said.

"Excuse me?" Nicky asked.

"I said, get the hell out of here," the man said. He started walking toward them.

"That's not how this works," Ken said, putting his hands on his gun. "We're here to—"

The man gave them a glare so full of malice, it felt like a physical form.

Nicky and Ken didn't give him a second glance. Talking to this guy was pointless, and there were other people in the park. The two of them turned away and walked over to the nearest trailer. Another group of men were standing outside of it, and the two of them stepped up to them. The group of men were just as intimidating, just as muscular, and just as tattooed.

"Hey, who are you?" one of the men asked.

That was when Nicky noticed that the previous group of men were now behind them, closing them in.

"They're with the FBI," the red-bearded man said. "They're looking for Prat."

The men looked at each other, and it seemed to Nicky like the trailers shook. The tension in the air was so thick, she could feel it. It was like the men were seconds away from beating the hell out of her and Ken.

"Is Prat here?" Nicky asked.

"Yeah," one of the men said. "He's here. Go ahead and look for him."

Nicky nodded. "Thank you."

She turned to Ken. "Time to go."

But the men didn't let them leave. Instead, they surrounded Nicky and Ken. Nicky felt her heart leap in her chest. These guys were bad news—and Nicky had a feeling they didn't care if they were here on FBI business or not.

It seemed like the people in this trailer park protected their own.

Around them, more crowds had gathered, spectating. There were at least fifty people in the trailer park.

Another man stepped forward. He was short and stocky, with a black goatee. "Hey, FBI bitch," he said. Nicky's teeth clenched. "We had a little chat. It seems like you're looking for Nial Prat. Well, listen good, 'cause we don't need to repeat ourselves. Nial's not here. He's not gonna talk to you. So scram."

The men around Nicky didn't say anything as they formed a circle around her and Ken. Nicky felt her scalp tighten.

"You're making a mistake," Nicky said.

Ken reached for his gun. "Let us through. I'm not asking, I'm telling. We're here to do a job, and you can't stop us."

"I don't think you understand," one of the men said, his voice rising. "You're not gonna find Prat here."

"Well, I think we better go look for ourselves," Nicky said. "We're federal agents. You're interfering with an investigation."

The men laughed. "What are you going to do? Shoot us? Screw you."

Nicky took a deep breath. She was prepared to draw her gun if she had to. In the past, situations like this had usually ended with an arrest. Or something worse.

But if Nicky was going to get answers, she was going to have to get through all of these men. She couldn't act irrationally—she had to save face. It was the only way to win.

The men swayed, putting their hands on their hips and on their knives. They were all looking at Ken and Nicky with a mixture of amusement and derision, like they were all wondering how long it was going to take to break these two.

Nicky could feel her heart pounding in her chest. She hated how powerless she felt. All of these men were just waiting for a reason to pounce. Nicky didn't want to resort to gun violence, and she flipped through her mind for the best way to handle this. It seemed like talking her way out of it would be best.

"You're making a mistake," Nicky said. "I'm not going to ask you again."

"Yeah, you are," the stocky man said. "You're going to ask us a lot before this is over. You're going to ask for our help."

The crowd laughed.

"When you do," the man said, "we're going to give it to you. With a knife in your belly."

The men raised their hands and made a blade with their fingers. Nicky swallowed down the lump in her throat. She had to get out of there.

But just then, over the crowd, Nicky heard the door to a trailer slam shut.

She looked over to see a heavyset man—one who matched the description of Nial Prat—making a run for it.

"There!" she said, pointing him out.

Nicky and Ken pushed through the crowd, fighting their way forward. The laughing crowd was thick and intent on the show in front of them. Up ahead, through the gaps in the people, Nicky could see Prat as he dodged left and right to get out of the park.

He was getting away.

CHAPTER TWENTY THREE

The crowd was surging with excitement, but Nicky didn't care—she just needed to get through, no matter what it took. She turned to Ken, who nodded back at her, and then both of them took off at a run. Nicky felt her head starting to throb, but she wasn't going to give up this time.

What the kidnapper had said before; it had some truth to it. No matter how it was spun, Nicky did leave Rosie behind. She didn't care if she was just a scared kid—she'd still left her sister with that madman, and it had haunted her every day since.

The last thing she'd do was leave these other girls.

But the crowd was hellbent on keeping them here. A shoe was thrown at Nicky, and it bounced off her shoulder. Someone stuck their leg out in an attempt to trip Ken, but he jumped over them. The crowd was relentless in their pursuit, and Nicky and Ken found themselves being pelted by objects and food.

Prat ran and ran, and Nicky and Ken found themselves running through the trailer park as fast as they could. Nicky pushed through, dodging around foot traffic and jumping over fallen food. This was exactly what she didn't want today, and she was actually a little angry at herself for getting caught up in the moment; they should have been more discreet, coming into this place like this.

Prat was a big guy, lumpy, with a potbelly and a round face. He was wearing a green vest over a yellow shirt, and he ran like he didn't even know that Nicky and Ken were following him.

He was the lowest link. He would have been easy to catch, if not for the citizens getting in the way.

Nicky felt like she was in a dream. Things moved so fast around her, and she could barely keep up with them. Her heart ached from the effort of running, and her lungs started to burn, but she kept moving forward.

She was so intent on chasing Prat that she didn't see the woman coming around the corner. Nicky slammed into her, and the two of them fell to the ground.

106

The woman pushed herself up and started yelling curses at Nicky, but Nicky didn't even hear her. She got back to her feet and kept running, with Ken close behind her.

"There he is!" Ken said, pointing ahead.

Nicky saw Prat. He was still running, but he wasn't getting out of the park. He was heading in the opposite direction, away from the exit. He was too distracted to notice them, and he was completely unaware that they were closing in on him.

Prat pushed through another crowd of people. A moment later, he rounded a trailer, and Nicky and Ken quickly followed.

Ken was still behind her. The two of them were working as a team, now, and that's what kept them going. "Keep moving, Lyons," Ken said. "We've got this bastard."

Nicky gritted her teeth. She wouldn't give up.

That's when Nicky felt someone grab onto her from behind. She struggled, but it was too late; the person was strong and they grabbed onto her arms. She felt her insides tense up.

"FBI!" she shouted.

The person who was grabbing her had a firm grip. She felt his fingers dig into the fabric of her clothing, and the pain was reaching her.

"Let go of me!" Nicky shouted.

She felt Ken come up next to her. For a moment, the two of them struggled against the crowd, trying to move away.

That was when Nicky noticed who'd grabbed her.

The red-headed man.

His green eyes blazed in the sun.

The sound of the gunshot reverberated through the air. The man dropped Nicky. She scrambled away from him, her hands grazing the ground, and stood next to Ken.

The man's hands flew up and he backed away, all the other people in the crowd following, their hands in the air. Ken was pointing his gun at them all, watching them carefully to make sure they didn't move too quickly. A cloud of smoke waved through the air, drifting past Ken's face and into his eyes,

"What the hell did you do?" Nicky asked.

"Fired a warning shot into the air," Ken said. Slowly, they backed away from the crowd, who now seemed to realize what they were doing.

"We're with the FBI," Nicky said, "and if you continue to interfere with our investigation, each and every person here will be charged with assaulting a federal officer. I highly suggest each of you return to your homes."

The crowd grumbled, but Nicky could see the expressions on their faces; they weren't going to keep pushing. She could tell that most of them didn't have any idea what was going on.

They were just people, trying to get by, and the last thing they needed was a bunch of FBI agents walking into their lives demanding answers.

Nicky relaxed.

Finally, she had the chance to catch her breath.

She felt lightheaded, like she was going to collapse, and her head was throbbing something awful.

Slowly, the men and women in the crowd started to disperse. It was like a tide, receding back onto itself and leaving nothing but silence behind.

Nicky turned around, and she could see that Prat had run off and was out of sight. She could still see a few people walking away, but they kept their heads down, afraid to look back.

Nicky nodded at Ken. "He went that way. Let's go."

They took off again, their feet pounding the pavement. Nicky and Ken were in top shape, and chasing down a perp was just another day for them. Although Prat had a good head start on them, it wasn't long before they rounded a corner and saw him rushing into a field.

Nicky ran through the blaze of the sun, following Prat's figure as he darted this way and that. He was moving faster than she had expected him to, but he looked tired.

After a quick sprint, Nicky closed the distance between her and Prat. Prat must have felt her coming, because he turned around, saw Nicky, and froze.

He had a big, round face and a bald head. His eyes were as brown as the dirt under their feet.

Nicky grabbed his shoulder. He tensed up. "Where are the girls?" she demanded.

"Get off me!" Prat cried.

"Where are they!?"

Prat, with all his might, pushed Nicky away, and she went flying back. She hit the ground, and a bolt of pain shot through her bones.

108

"You're messing with the wrong guy, lady," Prat said. "I'll say it right now; I ain't talking to you."

He reached into his pocket and pulled out a pair of brass knuckles.

Prat slid them onto his hand, ready to fight.

Nicky rolled over and got back to her feet. She felt a sharp pain in her side, but she kept it together.

"You're going to talk," she said.

Prat glared at her. He was breathing hard, but he stood his ground. "You think this is the first time I've run from the cops?" he asked.

"I think you're going to tell me where those girls are," Nicky said.

"Screw you."

Nicky charged at him, and the two of them slammed into each other. Prat was heavier than Nicky, but she was much faster. She dodged his first punch and rammed her elbow into his face.

Prat raised his hands, blocking Nicky's second blow. His brass knuckles collided with her fist, and the impact sent sparks flying.

Nicky winced. That was when Ken caught up, gun out.

"FBI!" he shouted.

Prat turned around as he heard Ken's voice. Nicky grabbed his arm, twisted it behind his back, and slammed him into the ground.

"Where are the girls?" Nicky demanded. She put all her weight behind her knee and drove it into Prat's back. "Where are they!?"

"Nobody's here!" Prat said.

She pressed her knee harder into his back. "I will break every bone in your body if you don't tell me the truth!"

"I swear!" Prat said. "I don't know what you're talking about! You've got the wrong guy."

Nicky reached into her pocket and took out a pair of handcuffs. She slammed them onto Prat's wrists, then pulled him to his feet.

"You're coming with us," she said.

CHAPTER TWENTY FOUR

Nicky dragged Prat into the local precinct's interrogation room—a cold, sterile box of a room. She shoved him, handcuffed, into a chair and then sat down in front of him. Ken came in and sat beside her.

"I want to know where those girls are," she said. "If you don't tell me, I can make your life very difficult."

Prat glared at her, his eyes darting around the room and then settling on her face. His face was sweating, and his hands were shaking.

"I don't know anything," he said.

"I think you do," Nicky said. "And I think you're going to tell me what you know. If you don't, I'll make sure you go away for a very long time."

Prat shook his head and his face became red. His whole body was trembling. Nicky could tell he was lying to her, but she didn't care. She only cared about getting those girls back.

"I didn't kidnap any girls," Prat said. "You're out of your goddamn mind, lady."

Nicky wasn't buying it. This sack of shit sitting in front of her could easily be the same guy she'd talked to on the phone. She didn't trust him for a second.

"Tell me where they are, Prat," she uttered, "and maybe we can cut you a deal, give you a lighter sentence. The girls are still alive, right? That's just kidnapping, not murder. So you should really start talking."

He rolled his eyes, like this was all a joke to him. "Look, I told you already, I didn't take no girls."

Nicky was getting sick of this. She took out her phone and pulled up the photo of the dolls, shoving it in Prat's face. "You recognize these dolls?"

He squinted. "No? I don't play with no dolls."

"Bullshit." Nicky slapped the table. "You purchased these from Cynthia's Dolls, Nial. You better start telling the truth."

He leaned back in the chair, a look of recognition crossing his face. "Oh, yeah… them dolls. Yeah, I bought them, but I also bought a bunch of other shit. I have yard sales. I sell lots of junk there.

Sometimes I buy kids' shit so it'll draw in the parents, then hope they'll buy my other stuff."

Nicky didn't buy it. If he was the guy she spoke to on the phone, then everything was a game to him. He couldn't be trusted.

"Tell me where the girls are, Nial," Nicky demanded.

"I don't know! Seriously! I don't know nothing about any kidnapping! Check my record! I ain't got no priors!" He was lying through his teeth and Nicky knew it.

"If those girls are hurt and we can't find them, I'm going to make sure you feel a whole lot of pain."

Prat's eyes widened. "That's not me! I bought some dolls a while ago, but that's all I know! I swear!"

"We'll see."

That was when the door burst open. Two people wearing identical black suits walked briskly into the room. Nicky had never seen them before. The woman's face was beautiful, but serious and cold. She wore her long blonde hair in a tight bun. The man, who had close-cropped black hair, was taller by at least a foot. He had a close-shaven beard and mustache.

Nicky's stomach fell. She could practically smell that they were feds.

Which could only mean that this case—it was evolving out of Nicky's hands.

She wasn't acting fast enough.

No, she thought, this is my case. I can do this, I can—

"Agent Lyons, Agent Walker," the man said. "I'm Special Agent Eric Burke and this is my partner, Special Agent Nicole Farris. Is this the suspect?"

"Oh, goodie," Nial said, "more suits."

Nicky was completely put on the spot. She stammered, "We're in the middle of an interrogation."

"Well," Eric said, "we were sent here to help survey the situation. Turns out Mr. Prat here has a storage locker, and the police are on their way to search it now."

Suddenly, Prat went pale. "Wait, no—you can't go there!" He looked horrified. He pushed back his chair, but before he could escape, Ken hopped up and restrained him. "You'll be staying right here, friend."

"Stop it! That storage locker is my property! You can't do this!"

"Sit down," Ken demanded, shoving down on Nial's shoulders so he was forced to sit on the chair. He stood beside Nial to keep watch in case he tried to stand up again.

Nicky stood up, facing the two new agents. "I'm in charge of this investigation, Special Agent Burke. I have it under control. What exactly are you here for?"

"We're here to assess the scene and determine if there's something we should be doing in addition to the regular tasks," Eric said. "I'm sure you're doing a fine job."

She heard the mocking in his tone. He didn't think she was capable of handling the case, but she wouldn't let him push her out of it.

"I appreciate the help, but this case is mine, and I'm going to bring those girls home."

"It seems like you could use the extra hands," Nicole added.

Nicky was fuming. They were undermining her, right in front of a perp. She didn't care if they had earned the title of special agent—this was her case. But there was nothing more she could do without losing her professional demeanor.

Nicky sat back down in the chair. "Well, you two are welcome to spectate as I get the truth out of this bastard."

Nial gave her a cheeky smile, which Nicky wished she could slap right off him.

"So, Nial," Nicky said, "since the police are on their way anyway, why don't you tell us the truth about what's in that storage locker?"

"It sure as hell isn't kidnapped girls, I'll tell ya that much," Nial said. He shot Nicky a wink. "Maybe I should talk to those other two fine special agents over there instead of you, huh, sweetheart? Seems like you're a bit in over your head…"

Nicky clenched her teeth. But it wasn't Nial she was frustrated with—it was Burke and Farris. They could have talked to her privately, and now her own suspect didn't respect her authority.

"As I said, I'm in charge of this investigation," Nicky said, "and I'm in charge of you too, Nial. You won't be getting out of those handcuffs anytime soon. Start talking."

He grinned. "Aw, I know you're just excited to hear me talk, baby. Maybe later, when you're in your bed, if you're really good, I can give you a call and we can talk some more…"

Nicky was fuming. She wanted to grab Nial by his long hair and bash his face in. But she had to stay composed. He was trying to push her buttons. To see how she'd react. She wouldn't give him the satisfaction of reacting.

"Is that what you told the girls when you kidnapped them?" Nicky shot back.

But Nial just shrugged. "I didn't kidnap any girls. You really are wasting your time. The real guy's out there, and it ain't me."

"We'll see about that."

Just then, the door opened up, and an officer poked his head in. He waved for the agents to meet him in the hall. Shooting one last fiery glance at Nial, Nicky, along with Ken, Eric, and Nicole, all met with the officer in the hallway.

"What's going on?" Nicky asked, keeping her voice loud so she would not be overpowered by Eric or anyone else.

"Well... I just got a call," the cop said. "Prat's locker—it's all full of stolen junk. But there's no girls there."

Nicky's heart fell into a pit. "Could he be holding them anywhere else?"

"There's nothing else in his name. No vehicles, nothing."

"Not an ATV?" Nicky asked, gaining a look from Burke and Farris.

"No," the officer said. "He's just got his trailer, and besides, people say they've seen him around non-stop for the past week... a client for one of his odd construction jobs accounted for him too."

"So," Eric cut in, "it seems unlikely he would be able to pull this off."

The officer shrugged. "The guy's a bad seed, but... I sort of doubt it. He's not exactly a criminal mastermind. We all know him here."

Nicky looked at Burke and Farris. They were looking at her as if waiting to see what she decided to do. She could feel their eyes on her, scrutinizing her. They didn't think she could handle this case. And so far, she really wasn't proving them wrong. She knew she needed to do something to prove them wrong, to show them she was the boss and deserved to be in charge. To show them that she was smart, she knew how to handle a case, she was a good agent.

But what did Nicky really want?

Remember, she told herself. You wanted this case. You wanted to make a difference. You wanted to help these kidnapped girls.

"I understand," Nicky said, glancing at Ken, who had a sympathetic look on his face. She turned away. "We have other leads to run down, so we'll be in touch."

With that, Nicky and Ken began to walk away. But as she did, Eric called after her, "We'll be in touch too, Agent Lyons, with what we find."

Nicky bit her tongue as she walked away.

Like hell would anyone take this case from her.

And like hell would anyone die under her watch.

It was back to the drawing board.

CHAPTER TWENTY FIVE

It was a different motel room, but Nicky felt the same as she did back in cottage country; like she was banging her head on the wall, looking for answers that just weren't there.

Once again, she had her laptop open in front of her. This motel, just outside of Rockwood, was at least a bit nicer than the last. The room was much warmer, the walls painted a warm orange that looked almost like a sunset, and the mattress was soft, like a well-used cloud. But Nicky sat alone at the table while Ken was across from her, looking into things on his own laptop.

They hadn't spoken much. There was too much pressure. The air was thick with it, and it surrounded them wherever they went, like a cloud of gnats that buzzed at the corner of their eyes and ears. Only the bedrooms were really quiet from the pressure, and no one wanted to be alone with only their thoughts for company. But it wasn't really her who held the weight of not two, not four, but six lives in her hands. It was Ken too. There was no way they could both make the decision on their own. Nicky hoped Ken didn't feel too much guilt over this, because in the end, Nicky was the leader; it was her job to save them.

Maybe the other two agents would do a better job. But Nicky wouldn't give up. She knew she was missing something huge that would tie this all together—she just hadn't figured it out yet.

She was now directing her attention to the newest victims: Ella and Emma Sorenson.

They, like the other girls, were twenty years old, and twins. They'd gone missing from a vacation home just about an hour from where Nicky and Ken were now—which told her that the kidnapper, most likely, was somewhere in the middle of all these towns. But where?

Nicky looked at a photo of Ella and Emma in their file and felt a pang of guilt. They were blonde-haired and freckled, with blue eyes. They looked different from all the other twins, but like the other two sets, one was a bit shorter and stouter, while the other appeared more athletic.

Nicky looked up their background info.

The girls' parents had divorced when they were young. Both girls went to a local university and were working part-time jobs while taking online classes. They were active in their university's theater program, and Ella had even won an acting award.

The files stated that they'd been out jogging the morning of their disappearance, and had not been heard from since, but another jogger had found the dolls and called the police, as they'd heard about the story on the news.

Nicky sighed. What wasn't she seeing?

She lifted her eyes from her laptop to see Ken across from her, staring.

"What is it?" she asked.

He took a breath. "Just... wanted to say I'm sorry about earlier."

Nicky clammed up. She figured he was referring to how the special agents had come in there and made her feel—and look—foolish and incapable of doing her job.

"They were just doing their jobs," Nicky said.

"Well, they don't have to act that way," Ken said. "I know they're the top dogs, and they've got a lot vested in their agents... but they can be more respectful."

Nicky felt surprised at Ken's words. "Well, thanks, Walker," she said. "I appreciate that."

He nodded.

"We really do need to stay focused," Nicky said, feeling awkward.

"I know," Ken said. "I just want you to know they shouldn't have talked to you like that."

She sighed. "Listen, I know I've made some mistakes with this case, but—"

"You haven't," Ken cut in. "You've been doing a great job on this case. I know you have it in you."

"Thanks," she said. She felt a swell of pride—Ken's words warmed her heart. But then she had to be honest. "I just wish I didn't have to make so many mistakes."

"You're not the only one working this case, Lyons," Ken said. "I'm older. Hell, I'm more experienced. I can't crack it either. This isn't all on you. We're gonna find them together."

A lump formed in Nicky's throat. It was good to hear. She really needed to hear it. She needed to hear it from someone—or even just herself, maybe. But Ken's words gave her hope; they were like a beacon of light in a black sea of despair.

Nicky nodded. "Thank you."

"No," Ken said, shaking his head. "Thank you. For having my back."

Nicky felt her cheeks grow warm. "That's my job," she said.

She checked the clock: it was past lunch. She could smell the fat from the fried noodles from the restaurant across the parking lot. But neither of them had any appetite.

Ken pointed to her computer. "So, how's it going?"

Nicky looked at the files. "Still too much—twins, families with divorced parents, drama at school… it's all too commonplace. There's gotta be something else."

Something that could link all these twins together…

Nicky decided to go back to the original two: London and Paris Knight. Their parents were Chad Knight and his wife, a Danish immigrant named Freja Knight, nee Rasmussen. However, according to the file, Freja was not big on the customs of her home country and loved to travel, hence the names of her daughters: London and Paris.

Then there were the Millers, Susie and Sammy. Their father was Dan Miller, and their mother was Josefine Miller, nee Pedersen.

Nicky paused.

Wait a second…

Ella and Emma Sorensen—their last name was distinctly Danish.

London and Paris's mother was quite literally from Denmark.

Nicky looked further, into the Miller girls. Susie and Sammy—their mother also had a Danish maiden name.

"Ken…" Nicky trailed off.

"What is it?"

"I think I found it." She didn't want to get ahead of herself, but this was too huge to ignore. She looked up at Ken and met his eyes, determined. "I think I found the link. All of the girls have Danish backgrounds."

It was Ken's turn to look at her, dumbfounded.

"You're right," he said. "They do."

"The Sorensens are Danish," Nicky continued. "Mr. Knight's wife was Danish, and so is the mother of the Millers."

Ken widened his eyes. "Holy shit," he said. "It's all of them. All the girls have Danish parents or a Danish connection."

Nicky realized this could be a blessing and a curse. On one hand, they had a link. On the other, they had no actual clue as to why.

"What does this mean?" Ken asked.

Nicky's mind was racing. "I think it could allude to the identity of the kidnapper. Maybe he's from Denmark, and that's why he's choosing these girls."

"Or it could be that he's trying to connect with someone from Denmark," Ken said.

"Maybe a relative," Nicky said. "Either way, the Danish connection could be very important. I think we should include this in our profile."

"Right," Ken said. "Yeah, absolutely. This is huge."

Nicky leaned back in the chair. "I feel like a weight has been lifted."

"Me too," Ken said. "We're gonna get these girls home."

Nicky wanted to believe it. But she knew she had to be realistic. There was a long road ahead, with many more twists and turns. There was no way to know exactly what horrors the girls might endure now, or when they'd be found, if ever.

But Nicky knew that if there was one thing she could control, it was her own actions. And all she had to do was keep scouring every second of video footage, every file on the victims, everything she could get her hands on, until they could find these girls.

There was no way she was giving up.

CHAPTER TWENTY SIX

As the day ticked on through the window of the motel room, Nicky spent the next hour building up a solid profile of the killer.

One thing she was assuming was that he was Danish, or the child of an immigrant with a strong connection to their heritage. His obsession with girls of this lineage seemed to point to that, maybe. Nicky couldn't prove it yet—but she had nothing else to go on. He was probably a single male. Owned an ATV.

This had to narrow down the list.

But with every second spent, it was another second closer to all six girls losing their lives. They needed to find this guy. There was not a single moment to spare, and so Nicky, on a whim, sent the profile to every single person connected to the case. The girls' parents. The officers in local towns. Even Cynthia, the toy store owner.

Every single person.

She didn't care who, and she wasn't going to hold anything back. She was desperate. Desperate for a lead. Desperate for this to not be another dead end.

Nicky wanted to see if she could get into the girls' minds and know exactly what they saw and felt at the moment of their disappearance. She had seen a few times that there were often moments of great clarity, and she wanted to see if she could get into that place.

As they waited for something—anything—to come in, Nicky leaned back in the chair and closed her eyes. She imagined that day again; the day she and Rosie had been taken, all those years ago.

But not only that.

She thought about the days that followed, after she'd gotten away from the kidnapper. After the police had told her that they couldn't locate her sister.

And then the days after that, when she'd first gone to school. The police had told her that there was a chance that Rosie wasn't alive anymore. And it had been a terrifying time.

She'd been so alone.

After the days of feeling terrified and alone, not knowing if Rosie was alive or dead.

The day she saw her again—in a vision, when she was still terrified. The visions she had of being back in that cabin with Rosie, back at that lake house. The calm, rippling water. How it had calmed her, in a sick way.

These visions changed her life—they led her to the right path, to the right decisions. They inspired her to become an FBI agent. But they had also haunted her in a way, and she always thought they would be the final ghosts of her past.

Do I really have to go through this again?

Nicky felt the familiar chill of dread sweep over her body.

But she knew this was something that had to be done. She knew that if she could get some insight into the kidnapper's head, she might be able to track him down.

It was a long shot, but it was all she had.

Nicky closed her eyes, trying to relax. How does a man like him think?

She tried to see the world through his eyes. She tried to think as he might, as he would. She tried to get into his mind. What could he possibly want with these girls?

She imagined a life like that; just being alone, with no one to talk to, with no friends.

Nicky imagined she was alone.

She imagined it was dark and cold.

But something could cure the loneliness. You can just take what you want.

It was all a game to him.

With the girls, he was in control. He could take what he wanted. Get off on it.

But getting off on it wasn't enough.

What did he really want?

Nicky felt herself sink deeper into the mind of a kidnapper. It didn't feel like she was in control anymore. It felt like she was in a trance.

She could hear the voices of people calling out to her.

She could feel their eyes on her, but she didn't care.

Nicky had never been a religious person, but now she felt like she was being pulled into some sort of religious experience.

Then, in the distance, she heard a voice.

Help me...

Nicky's eyes flew open.

But the voice went away.

She looked over at Ken, who was absorbed in his work—just as her phone, face-up on the table, vibrated. Heart in her throat, Nicky immediately snatched it up. It was a local number, but one she didn't recognize. She answered immediately: "This is Agent Nicky Lyons."

"A-Agent Lyons?" a voice stammered on the other end. "Um—it's Claire."

"Claire?" Nicky frowned, meeting Ken's confused gaze across the table. Claire, the single mom of Jacob, the little boy who'd heard the ATV. What did she want?"

"How are you, Claire?" Nicky asked. She put the phone on speaker so Ken could hear. He leaned his elbows on the table, listening intently.

"Um—that email you sent, with the information about who you think the kidnapper is?"

Nicky's heart picked up. "Yes?"

"The description, it... it made me think of someone I knew once. An ex-boyfriend, actually."

"Oh," Nicky said. She could hardly keep the slow-burning hope out of her voice. "Tell me about him."

"So I checked some things, and it seems like it could be him. He... he's single still, works at a warehouse, and has an ATV he's always riding around on. I just completely forgot about him until I saw your email."

"Did you date him for long?"

"About a month," Claire said. She sounded nervous. "But I never really trusted him. He's... he's a really big guy. He's really loud. Gave me the creeps sometimes. And then one day he just disappeared, and I never saw him again."

Nicky felt a chill run up her spine.

It can't be.

I might have just found the guy.

"Did he... did he ever hurt you?" Nicky asked. Her eyes met Ken's again. His were wide and wild with excitement.

"No," Claire said. "He was never violent with me. But if I really think about it, there were times when I noticed him staring out the window in the kitchen. And as you know, that window faces the cottage Sammy and Susie were staying in. They weren't there at the time, so I didn't see a connection… but maybe he knew who lived there?"

"And was he Danish? Or did he have Danish parents?" Nicky asked.

"I think he said his dad came from Denmark," Claire said.

"Is there any chance he was an only child, who lived alone?"

"He lived alone," Claire said. "He was an only child."

"Did he ever talk about his family?"

"He never seemed to want to," Claire said. "When he was with me, he didn't want to talk about it at all."

"And one last thing, Claire," Nicky said. "How long ago did you date him?"

"About three months ago, I think? As you know, I live here at the cottage year-round, and he was sort of a drifter who came in."

"Good, Claire," Nicky said. "Now I just need his name."

"His name is Felix. Felix Andersen."

"Thank you, Claire," Nicky said. Her heart was beating hard, and she felt wild. Adrenaline was flooding her system, and she felt like jumping up and running around the room. "We'll be in touch."

"Okay," Claire said. "I'm glad to help."

Nicky ended the call and clutched the phone tightly in her hand. "We got him," Nicky said. It almost didn't feel real.

She imagined the girls being saved. She imagined the moment when Felix Andersen was arrested, the moment when he found out he'd been caught. Would he appear shocked? Indignant? Furtive? Then he would be properly led away, bundle of lies and sadism, his despicable life reduced to a scribble on a single sheet of paper. It was a dirty business; she had taken an oath to uphold the law and she planned to do just that.

Felix thought he could force Nicky to play a game. But Nicky wasn't quick to let herself lose.

CHAPTER TWENTY SEVEN

Nicky walked up to the team of local police, waiting on the edge of a forest between Rockwood and the cottages, about an hour away from both. They stood in a line, wearing bulletproof vests, each of them holding an assault rifle as if they were going to war. It was a middle location, and here, a residence that was registered to Felix Andersen was somewhere in the forest.

It was later in the day now, and the sun was setting, creating an orange glow over the scene. Soon, night would fall, blanketing the world in darkness. Maybe that would be better for sneaking up on Felix's hideout.

An officer came up to Nicky and asked, "What are your orders, ma'am? Should we go in?"

Nicky thought on it. If all of these cops went into the forest, it would increase the likelihood of Felix noticing them. They needed to be tactful and quiet—first, locate the building, then send the team in. Their top priority was keeping those girls safe, and one wrong move could be life or death for them.

Nicky was still hatching her plan when a black car rolled up, and out came Special Agent Eric Burke and Special Agent Nicole Farris. Nicky's stomach fell. Not them.

Burke removed his sunglasses as he walked up to Nicky, Ken, and the officer. Nicole was quiet behind them, but she had a steely look in her eyes.

"Good work, Agent Lyons," Eric said. "Sounds like this might really be our guy."

Nicky nodded. "It seems that way."

"What's your plan of operation?"

Put on the spot, Nicky had to go with her gut: "Agent Walker and I will go in alone—we can't tip him off. We need air support, but helicopters would be too loud; if we could have drones following us and surveying the scene, then you can all monitor what's happening and help us locate the building. Special Agents Burke and Farris—I'm sure you will know when to send the police in."

Eric nodded. This time, there were no looks of judgment on his face—he seemed to accept Nicky's plan with no qualms, because he said, "That sounds good. Farris, get the drones set up."

"Understood." Nicole nodded and walked off toward the police paddy wagon parked nearby.

Nicky turned to the officer, still waiting for direction. "Please relay the plan to the others."

He nodded and walked off, leaving Nicky and Ken alone with Eric.

"Lyons, Walker," Eric said. "If you think you're going to need our help, don't be afraid to ask. We're not here to breathe down your necks. We're here to make sure this mission is a success."

Nicky nodded. She wanted to seem capable and in control, even if in truth, she was probably just as nervous as she'd been on her first mission. She glanced at Ken, who was quiet, and she could feel him on edge, his body tense.

Nicky turned. She saw Nicole Farris in a headset, directing the drone in the sky.

She watched it weave in the air, scanning the forest as if it were a search beam. Soon, they would enter the forest and hopefully find the building Felix was using to hold the girls.

Nicky imagined them huddled together. Their terror and sorrow. She imagined Felix in his hideout, waiting for them, ready to make his move.

She thought back to her training sessions at the FBI Academy. She remembered the challenges she had to face there—a surprise attack in a parking lot, an undercover operation where she'd had to infiltrate an anti-government group. Her pulse started to quicken. She felt a strange mix of fear, excitement, and adrenaline.

Focus, Nicky. She shut out everything else and prepared herself.

Looking at Ken, she gave him a nod, and he nodded back.

As Nicky walked into the woods, she knew that every moment on this investigation was leading to this.

She couldn't mess it up.

She couldn't let this man slip through her fingers.

She had to catch Felix.

***

The forest darkened as the sun set, and the shadows were long. Dirt and leaves crunched under her feet, and the canopy was thick above, blocking out the last of the light. There was a certain smell in the air, an olfactory sensation that told Nicky that she was in a place not meant for people—that this was a place that belonged to the animals of the night. Felix's cottage was somewhere in here.

Nicky was alert and ready. She was focused on the task at hand— and yet, she couldn't help but think of Felix.

What will I say to him? she thought. What will I say when I finally meet him?

There was a strange feeling in her stomach, something she wasn't used to feeling. It was a kind of urgency, and she didn't know what it meant. She'd never felt this way before when she'd arrested people— the sense that she was very close to something important, something that would change her life forever—but she couldn't help feeling that way now. She felt as if every moment was significant, and every step she took was leading her to a moment she could never have imagined. A moment she couldn't wait for.

Or a moment she was afraid of.

Because this man, Felix—if he was their guy... then he might genuinely know something about the man who had taken Nicky and Rosie.

She could hear Ken behind her. He was keeping up, and he was being quiet. He was good at that; she knew that about him. That deep down, he was a good guy.

Nicky and Ken walked for about a half hour, and at one point, Nicky heard a branch crack. She motioned for Ken to stop. She didn't say anything, just listened in the darkness. They were probably close, but the location was unclear.

Until Nicky's radio buzzed. She picked it up and pressed a button, allowing Eric's voice to come through: "Lyons, are you there? Over."

"Special Agent Burke, I'm here," Nicky said, "over."

"Good. The drones spotted two locations, two different structures. We don't know which one is his, or if they both are. About a half mile apart. One of them is straight east of your location—the other is west."

Nicky's stomach sank. This was a risk she hadn't anticipated, but now it was real, and she was forced to devise a new plan of operation on the spot. She looked back at Ken, and he looked at her, waiting for orders.

125

"Copy that. We'll check them both out," Nicky said into the radio, "over."

"Good luck," Eric said, "Over and out."

Nicky looked at Ken. "We'll split up," she said. "I'll take one, you take the other."

She thought she saw Ken nod in the darkness, although his silence was heavy.

"Stay on the radio," Nicky said, putting in her earpiece. Ken did the same. They both had one, but only used it in times when they couldn't be together.

"I will," Ken said. But there was a moment of hesitation. "Lyons…"

"What is it?" Nicky asked.

"Just… be careful," Ken said. It sounded like he wanted to say more, but he didn't.

Nicky looked at him for a moment, and then nodded. "You too," she said. And with that, they went their separate ways.

Nicky's feet crunched on top of the forest floor. It was easy to lose the sense of the other person here. The forest was dense and dark. If Ken was going to keep moving and stay silent, he was probably going to be fine.

But what if he's not? Nicky thought.

She stopped in the darkness when a glint of yellow showed through the trees. A light? She strained her eyes, but all she could make out was the yellow glint, which seemed to float in the darkness. A flashlight? She licked her lips. Or was it really a light? She froze and pulled out her gun. Then she heard a crackle of her earpiece. Was that Ken?

"Ken?" she whispered.

"Hey," came Ken's voice in her ear. "You okay?"

She looked around in the darkness, but nothing was there. Her heart pounded, and she wasn't sure if what she'd just witnessed had even happened. She felt as though eyes were upon her, watching her, judging her.

"I'm good, I just… thought I saw something."

"I'm on my way west. I'm right here if you need me."

Nicky kept moving through the Florida forest. She could hear a stream in the distance, and the trickling of the water, plus the darkness and trees surrounding her, brought her back to that horrible event from her past.

126

Don't think about it, she reminded herself. Focus. You've got this. You're almost there.

She kept moving through the trees, through the darkness.

CHAPTER TWENTY EIGHT

As Nicky continued through the forest, she felt like she was in a maze—although she didn't have the sense of being lost, but of being trapped. Caught. Trapped in the maw of a beast.

She kept walking, and the forest felt like it had no end. She could hear water in the distance, and there was something deep inside her that remembered the water, remembered what happened—the shock of the cold water and the hands on her body.

That was cut short by a sound.

A snap of a branch, and then the sound of a raspy breath. Someone was behind her, following her.

Nicky stopped. She waited, and then looked back.

She couldn't make out anything behind her. She kept her gun drawn and her finger on the trigger.

"Who's there?" she said.

There was no response. It must have been her imagination, she concluded.

Her mind playing tricks.

With the gun in her right hand, she said into her earpiece, "Ken?"

Alone out here, with all this darkness, she needed to hear his voice.

There was no response, which wasn't like him, and her anxiety returned in full force.

"Walker, come in, are you there?"

She waited.

A moment later, her earpiece crackled, and Ken said, "Lyons, I'm here. I'm at the second location. It's clear—no one's here. Just an old house with a rocker on the porch. But I also found an ATV."

Nicky's limbs went numb. This is it, she thought. If he wasn't at Ken's location, then that meant he was at the one Nicky was trying to find.

"Are you sure?" Nicky asked.

"Positive. No life here. Have you found the other location?"

"Not yet. I'm looking."

"I'll come find you."

Nicky moved out of the forest into a clearing. Her heart was pounding, and she had a sick feeling in her gut. She didn't know why, but she had a sense that this was it. They were at the end.

She searched the clearing, but there was nothing there. No sign of the other building. She looked back at the forest, and she couldn't shake the feeling that something was watching her, stalking her. She started to move back into the trees, and she heard the sound again. The snap of a branch, and then the raspy breath. Someone was definitely following her. Nicky stopped and looked back, but she still couldn't see anything in the darkness.

Her frustration—and paranoia—were growing. She needed to find the location. She took out her phone and checked her GPS location, which said she was just standing in the middle of the forest. She'd gone straight east, and she should have found the other building by now.

She took out her radio and pressed a button. "Special Agent Burke, are you there? Over."

"I'm here, Lyons. Over."

"Am I close to the second location? Over."

A drone whirred by in the night sky.

"Try moving a little to the north. We see something there. Not sure what it is. Over."

"Will do," Nicky said. "Over and out."

She moved up a slight slope, but the trees were so thick she could hardly see the sky. She kept moving, pushing through the trees, and she got on the other side of the hill, onto a more even surface. She went through a forest patch, with more trees, but then she saw something. An opening in the forest—a path that led to the right.

The path was narrow, but it was definitely there. And it looked like it had been used recently.

Nicky's heart quickened as she realized this must be the location. She started down the path, her gun drawn, and she radioed Ken. "I think I found it," she said.

"I'm on my way," Ken said.

Nicky moved down the path, her gun drawn. She was on high alert, and she didn't want to take any chances. She rounded a corner, and she saw it. A huge metal door set into the side of a hill. It was camouflaged to blend in with the surroundings, but there was definitely something there.

Nicky approached cautiously, her heart pounding in her chest. This could be it—the location of the missing people. She reached out and touched the door handle, half expecting it to be electrified or booby-trapped in some way. But it seemed safe, so she slowly opened the door and stepped inside.

It was pitch-black inside, and Nicky had to pause for a moment to let her eyes adjust. When they did, she saw that she was in some kind of bunker.

She took a step back. A sick smell was coming from the inky-black darkness, and Nicky hesitated. She couldn't just go in guns blazing.

She stepped back from the bunker and radioed in, whispering quietly: "Special Agent Burke, I've got eyes on a bunker. Send the police to my location, and send them quietly. Over."

A moment later, her radio crackled, and Eric said, "Ten-four. Officers inbound. Over and out."

She waited, but she didn't hear any sounds coming from the bunker. She glanced around the perimeter, but there was nothing to see.

Should I go inside? she thought.

The urgency was growing. She could feel the beast inside of her, the beast that had been whispering to her, telling her in its terrifying growl that it was time to act.

To do what?

To end this.

Then, suddenly, Nicky heard a crack in the darkness again. She whipped around, hearing sticks crunch.

Something was coming.

She tensed, ready to fight, but then she saw a figure emerge from the darkness.

Ken appeared between the trees.

Relief flowed through her, and Nicky relaxed.

"Jesus, Walker. You scared me."

"Sorry about that," he muttered, coming up to the bunker's entrance. "Any sign of life in there?"

Nicky looked into the pitch-black. "Nothing. But he has to be in there." She paused. "Walker, there's something wrong with this one. I have a bad feeling. I don't know what it is, but keep your gun out."

"You think he's armed?"

"Yeah, probably. It's that feeling I have, it's like I'm being watched. As if he's playing with us."

They moved into position—Nicky in front, and Ken to the side. They both crouched down, their guns in hand. Nicky didn't know what they would find in there. Ken nodded, and together, they moved in.

The bunker was musty and damp, and it took a moment for their eyes to adjust to the darkness. There were no windows, the only light coming in from the doorway behind them, where barely a sliver of moonlight reached them. Nicky would turn on her flashlight, but she didn't want to tip him off.

The first thing Nicky noticed was the smell. It was a mix of blood and death, and she had to fight the urge to gag. The hallway was a long corridor lined with what appeared to be cells.

Each one was empty and dark, but she could still see the stains on the walls and floors, and she knew exactly where the smell was coming from.

Nicky tried not to look too hard at those stains, but she couldn't help herself. The blood was spattered across the walls and the floor, and she followed it to the end of the corridor.

There was a small room, with a single bunk and a small toilet. The walls and floor were spattered with blood, as if someone had painted with it. As if he had been practicing his art.

Nicky felt her stomach turn. The place was a slaughterhouse, and she didn't want to think about what had happened here. But the blood—it all looked very old. Nicky crept into one of the cells and used the dim light from her phone to illuminate it. She touched her hand to the wall.

No, this wasn't blood...

It had the waxy feeling and chemical smell of wall paint.

What was this?

Nicky paused, taking a moment. Ken must have been looking in another cell, because she was alone here.

What was the purpose of making this place out to look like a slaughterhouse?

Was this another part of the kidnapper's sick game?

Maybe he wanted to scare them. Maybe he wanted them to think he was a monster, that the blood was fresh. But it wasn't. It was all very old.

Nicky thought, and then it hit her.

A sick feeling came over her.

She knew what this was.

It was another part of the game, but it wasn't just for Nicky.

It was for the missing people, too. He probably controlled them this way; he made them think that this was real blood, and that if they didn't obey them, he'd kill them like he'd killed others. But maybe he'd never really killed anyone at all.

He was controlling the people, making them think he was capable of murder, but in reality, he was just kidnapping people and making them stay down here. The whole thing was a game, a twisted game, and the police were just pawns in in. But maybe these six girls—he really did intend to kill them. Maybe they were his first real victims. He'd finally paint with real blood.

Nicky's skin crawled. The kidnapper had to be close, and she wanted to catch him just as much as she wanted to keep away.

Nicky kept moving, leaving this cell for the next. The cells were large, big enough to comfortably hold a group of people. But there was no comfort here. Each cell was a concrete box, with a high ceiling and no windows. The walls and floor were splattered with blood, and there was no bed.

There was a door at the very back of the corridor, and Nicky tiptoed over to it. She pressed her ear against the metal, and she heard some muffled sounds. Someone was in there, but she couldn't tell who. Or what.

She turned the handle and opened the door.

The room was dark, but she could just make out a figure sitting on the ground. Wait, no, not a figure—several figures. And there were whimpering sounds.

Nicky couldn't believe what she was seeing.

All six girls, chained up. Alive.

A man was in the room, holding a gun. He was pointing it at the girls, and they were whimpering in terror.

"I told you not to come down here," he said, his voice low and dangerous. "This is my game, and you're not supposed to be here."

Nicky's heart was pounding in her chest. She wanted to run, but she couldn't leave the girls.

"Please," she begged. "Just let them go. They haven't done anything wrong."

"They're not good enough for me," the kidnapper said. "And now they have to pay the price."

He cocked the gun and aimed it at one of the girls.

CHAPTER TWENTY NINE

Nicky's world froze. She couldn't think. Couldn't breathe.

But the kidnapper, Felix—he never fired the gun. It wasn't too late. Nicky had time, time to stall him. Time to fix this.

She lowered her own gun as Felix's blue eyes glared at her like silver in the darkness. She had to stall him, and one thing she knew about this guy was his heritage—and that it was apparently quite important to him, so important that he'd only chosen Danish victims.

Being an FBI agent, it was important to know several languages. Nicky's Danish was rusty, but she took a stab at it: "*Venligst lad være med at skyde...*" Please don't shoot.

Felix was immediately caught off guard. Nicky could see him clearer now: he was a tall, blond man with a narrow, leathery face. His eyes were cold as ice, and his mouth was a thin slash in his face.

Nicky continued in Danish, playing for time. "*Venligst, jeg er bare en rejsende. Jeg mener, du gør ingen skade.*" Please, I'm just a traveler. I mean you no harm.

She knew that was a ridiculous thing to say, but her Danish vocabulary was limited and she couldn't think of anything else. And there was a slim chance he'd actually believe she was just a random person who happened to stumble upon the situation.

Felix laughed. "*Bare rolig... jeg skydder dem alligevel.*" There, there... I'm going to shoot them anyway.

"*Det kan du ikke... jeg er først og fremmest kommet for at spørge dig om hjælp...*" You can't... First and foremost, I'm here to ask for your help.

Felix looked caught off guard, and he paused. "*Hjælp?*" he repeated.

Then he laughed and shook his head. "Foolish, aren't you? You think I'll fall for this, Nicky Lyons?"

Nicky stiffened. Damn it.

"I would never forget that beautiful, smooth voice of yours," he said. "You're clever, I'll give you that. But only so clever that you could get yourself in here and try to save these girls. You have no idea what I'm capable of, do you?"

"I know that you're not capable of murder," Nicky said. "All that blood covering the walls… it's paint."

Felix's eyes flashed, and for a moment, Nicky feared she'd gone too far. But then he laughed. "You're giving me more credit than I deserve. It's true, I don't like blood… but I wouldn't think twice about killing you. You've run out of time to stall," he said. "I'm going to start killing them."

A chill went down Nicky's spine. This guy was completely insane. He was going to kill them all, and she wasn't going to be able to stop him. The girls were in mortal danger, and she didn't know what to do.

"Okay," she said, "I'll play your game."

"Oh, you will, will you?" he taunted. "If that's the case, then did you decide which of these beautiful girls will die? Or will it be all six?"

Nicky's eyes flew to the girls. She knew she couldn't choose who would live and who would die. And yet, she had to choose…

There was no way out of this.

She hated Felix's game, and she hated him even more. She'd humiliated him once already, but this time… this time she was going to get him.

"Let them all live," she said.

"Let them all live?" He laughed, and he spun the gun in his hand, pointing it at the girls. "Why would I do that?" He turned the gun back to Nicky. "I could kill you right now, and then I'd have all the time in the world to do it. But I won't kill you yet, Nicky. I'll kill you later. I want to savor this moment—I want to savor *you*."

"You're bluffing! You might be crazy, but you're not cruel enough to kill all these innocent people," Nicky said. She didn't know for sure if that was true, but she was trying to get in his head. "That's why there's only paint on the walls. You've never killed before, Felix. You've thought about it, but you've never done it."

He made a twisted face. Maybe she was getting somewhere with this.

"I'm not bluffing," he said. "But here, I'll give you a choice. Choose one of them to die."

The girls were huddled together in the corner of the cell, crying, and Nicky's heart broke when she looked at them. How could she choose?

"I'll do it for you," he said. "Pick one."

Nicky didn't need to think about it. She knew whom she had to protect.

She took a step away from the girls, and she raised her gun to point at Felix. "You might be sick, but I'm not. I'm not going to help you hurt these poor girls."

Felix laughed, but he was visibly nervous. "Yes, you will. You're a desperate fool for getting yourself into this situation, and now you're a desperate fool for refusing to help me escape this situation. You just don't know when to quit, do you?"

Nicky glanced over her shoulder. Ken was in the bunker somewhere, but maybe he couldn't hear them. She didn't know where he was, but she hoped he'd get here soon. Felix didn't know he was here. And that could give them the ultimate upper hand.

But until then, she had to keep him talking. And there was one way, one personal way, she felt could actually get her out of this.

"You... you mentioned you know me," Nicky said.

Felix looked amused. "I know of your story, Nicky Lyons. I know of your sister, Rosie Lyons."

Her throat became straw-tight. "Is she alive? Do you know who took her?"

"Oh dear, do you think I would give you what you want, when you won't even give me what I want? You must choose a girl, Nicky."

"I won't," Nicky said. "I won't let you hurt them."

Felix grinned hugely. "Then let's bring this to a head, shall we?"

He turned the gun on the girls, the barrel pointing at one of the redhead twins. "I'm going to kill her, Nicky. Right now, I'm going to kill her."

Nicky's stomach dropped.

"You have to choose."

His finger was on the trigger. She could see it move.

She had to choose.

Nicky lowered her gun. "Okay."

"What did you say?"

"I said okay," Nicky said. "Whatever you want."

Felix wrinkled his face. "You're doing this of your own free will?"

"Yes," Nicky said.

"We're going to do this right now," he said. "No more delays. Which one will die?"

135

Nicky looked down at the six trembling girls, who all stared up at her, the whites of their eyes showing. She wouldn't pick one. She couldn't. But she stared at them all, drawing out the moment, so Felix would believe she was considering it.

But she was closer to him now.

It was a risk to all of them. Herself included. But Nicky had to take that risk—she had to fight.

Before he could even think about pulling that trigger, she lunged for him, slamming into him and knocking the gun out of his hand, sending it skittering across the floor.

Felix staggered back, and Nicky shoved him back against the wall and punched him in the face. She felt the sickening crunch of bone under her knuckles, and he yelled out in pain, covering his face with his hands.

"You insolent bitch!" Felix cried. He tackled Nicky to the ground, using his immense height and strength to overpower her.

He threw punch after punch at her, but she blocked and dodged as many of them as she could. When he pinned her down, she tried to wriggle free, but he was too big and too strong for her.

Soon, she was pinned against the floor, and she could feel his massive weight on top of her…

"No!" she yelled.

She was still alive, and she was still struggling. He was still trying to get to her.

He kept her pinned, his sweaty body pressed into hers. He held both of her arms above her head, but Nicky kneed him in the groin, causing him to retch in pain. But Felix quickly recovered, and the next thing Nicky knew, his fist came down hard on her face.

Nicky gasped. It felt like a thousand tiny wires were stabbing into her brain, ripping and tearing and burning. She howled in agony, in terror, in a pain so strong she couldn't describe it.

Slowly, the pain went away.

She opened her eyes and looked around the room.

She was surrounded by sand, standing on the shore of the lake house. Behind her was the cabin and the forest, but it was daytime this time. Sunlight sparked off the water in front of her, and she could smell the West Virginia forest.

The cabin door opened, and Rosie came out in a beautiful sundress.

"Hi, sis," she said. "It's so good to see you."

"Rosie..." Nicky breathed.

When her sister opened her arms, Nicky ran into them.

Rosie hugged Nicky tightly, and Nicky was so happy. She was warm and safe now, because her sister was here with her.

"I'm so sorry I didn't believe you," Nicky said. She wiped away a tear. "I'm so sorry you were taken, Rosie. I hope you can forgive me."

"There's nothing to forgive," Rosie said, pulling away. "I'm fine. I'm happy. I'm happy now. You found me."

"Where are we? Is this the way to the bunker?"

Rosie smiled. "Yes. We're almost there. Come on, Nicky."

She took her sister's hand and led her through the forest.

Nicky was so excited, but...

Something wasn't right.

There was something—someone—she was forgetting.

Rosie looked back at her with a beautiful smile. Long brown hair surrounded her slightly tanned face, and her brown eyes had never looked so full of life.

"My sister is alive," Nicky whispered to herself.

She was still alive. She hadn't given up. And Nicky would do everything in her power to be with her.

But what was she forgetting?

"Come on, Nicky," Rosie said. "Follow me. We can be together forever if you just follow me."

Nicky froze. The faces of six girls came back into her mind. "No... I... I can't."

Rosie paused, her expression saddening. "What do you mean?"

"I... I can't go with you," Nicky said. She felt the tears come to her eyes. "I'm sorry, Rosie. I'm so sorry."

Rosie looked hurt now. "Why? Why can't you come with me?"

"Because I have to save them," Nicky said.

"Save who?"

"The girls. I have to save them."

"No, Nicky," Rosie said, "don't leave me. You can't leave me again."

"I'm so sorry, Rosie," Nicky said. "I love you. I always have, and I always will. But I have to do this. You're not real, and they are..."

"No," Rosie said, starting to cry. "No, no, no..."

She dropped to her knees in the sand and buried her face in her hands.

Nicky swallowed, her throat like chalk. "Goodbye, Rosie."

Tears stung Nicky's eyes, and she turned and left her sister behind.

CHAPTER THIRTY

The dull, muffled sound of hard knuckles crashing into Nicky's face jarred her out of her sleep. Reality hit her harder than Felix's fist. The other girls screamed. The shock of it made her look up and realize that this wasn't a dream. She dodged out of the way as Felix's fist came down again.

Dodging another hit, she landed a glancing blow in his stomach and another on his face, but he only seemed to get angrier.

Nick spotted an opening and dove for the other side of the room where her gun had fallen. It was dark, and she couldn't see where it had landed. But Felix charged after her. As he did, one of the girls stuck a leg out and tripped him. He fell hard on the concrete floor and let out a howl.

He stumbled forward, and Nicky jumped to her feet, dodging behind him. The moment she had an opening shot, she slammed her gun into the back of his head. His head snapped forward then bounced back. He moaned, but she didn't hesitate. She hit him again, and this time he fell to the floor. Then she rolled him over and kicked him in the stomach. He screamed, and Nicky straddled him so she could throw a punch at his face. She trapped his arms in with her thighs and laid a punch on him, causing blood to spill. But he smiled up at her.

"Rosie," he whispered.

Rage struck her. How dare he say her name?

"Where is she!?" she demanded. "Who took her? Do you know him?"

He just laughed, spitting up blood.

Nicky grabbed him by the collar and shook him, but he was barely responding anymore. He just lay there, smiling up at the ceiling, whispering her sister's name over and over. "Rosie, Rosie, Rosie."

"Tell me where she is!" Nicky screamed. She couldn't take this. All Nicky could see was red. Pure, fiery hot red. Nicky punched him hard, and he finally he stopped moving entirely. Red blood poured from his nose.

Dead silence took over the room.

The girls were all staring at Nicky now. She was covered in blood. Her shirt was torn. It hurt to breathe.

"Is… is he dead?" one girl asked.

Nicky leaned over Felix's body. His eyes were closed, but his chest was still rising and falling. Nicky flipped him over and slapped cuffs on his wrists. "He's alive," Nicky said. "But he can't hurt you anymore."

She took a deep breath and stood up.

The girls stared at her.

"Who are you?" one of them asked.

"My name is Agent Nicky Lyons of the FBI," she said. "Are any of you hurt?"

The girls shook their heads, huddled in the corner. They were all bruised and battered, but they were alive. Nicky stared down at Felix's body. He had a black eye and a split lip. There was blood in his nose and a bruise on his forehead. He was lucky Nicky hadn't killed him.

"Did he hurt you while he kept you?" Nicky asked them.

The girls all exchanged looks, then shook their heads. "Not physically," one girl, whom Nicky recognized as Paris Knight, said. "He just kept us here… for so long…"

"He would torture us with games," another girl, who looked like Paris's sister, London, said.

"He'd give us a chance to escape," London said. "We'd be free for a few minutes, and we'd start to feel hope. But then he'd come find us and take it away…"

"He would do so many twisted things," said one girl, a red-headed twin whom Nicky was sure was Sammy Miller. "He'd try to make us choose between our sister's life and escaping, like he was trying to make you choose."

Nicky's heart sank. She knew what they meant. He had made them relive the same horror he had put her through. It had become unbearable to sit there and do nothing, watching helplessly as those girls suffered. Nicky knew she had to get her sister. She had to get her sister back.

First, she needed to finish this.

Nicky went to tap on her earpiece, but she realized it had fallen out in the chaos. Where on earth was Ken? She wanted to go find him, but she also didn't want to let these girls out of her sight. She took out her radio and pressed the button.

"Burke, I've got him. The hostages are safe and secured. We might need bolt cutters to free them. Where are the police? Over."

Burke's voice came in. "Roger that, Lyons—the unit should arrive in T-minus five minutes."

Nicky nodded to herself. Good. It was over.

We'll get you out of those chains," she said to the girls.

Suddenly, there was movement at the door, and Nicky looked up to see Ken's form in the doorway. "Jesus, what happened?" he said, surveying the scene. "I heard something outside and I went to look, then…"

"We got the guy," Nicky said. "It's done, Ken."

Ken let out a sigh of relief, and Nicky thought she saw a little bit of a smile.

"I'll get the girls out of their chains," Ken said. "Can you—"

She nodded. "I've got Felix. He's unconscious… but he's alive."

Ken was already getting to work on cutting the girls free. Nicky, meanwhile, hauled Felix's body up, still cuffed. She dragged him to the door, just as flashlights shone up the hall of the corridor.

"FBI!" Nicky shouted. "We're down here!"

The flashlight beams swung in her direction, and soon there were voices and footsteps coming toward them in the long corridor.

"Down here!" Nicky shouted again. The flashlight beams bobbed in her direction and came closer to her. Soon, police officers appeared around the corner, and Nicky let out a massive sigh of relief.

"Agent Lyons!" one of the officers called out.

"In here, hurry," she said.

Another officer with bolt cutters came in behind her. The officers took over the scene, freeing the girls and taking Felix into custody.

Ken came over to where Nicky was standing. "Are you okay?" he asked.

Nicky nodded. "I'm fine… The girls are fine…"

"You have blood on your face," Ken said.

Nicky touched her face and felt the wetness. Much of the blood wasn't hers. It was Felix's. But she'd done her job. The girls were alive, and Felix was going to pay for what he'd done.

"Well, I'm glad you're okay," Ken said.

Nicky nodded. She was glad she was okay too, but she was more glad that Ken was okay. She touched his arm, and he let out a breath. Nicky closed her eyes briefly, relieved. Then she opened them again and looked at Ken. With a sigh, Nicky looked down at her hands. She was covered in blood, and it was all over her uniform. At least it was Felix's blood…

"You did good, Lyons," Ken said.

"Yeah," she said. "But I'm not done yet."

EPILOGUE

Nicky stepped off the elevator into the FBI field office in Jacksonville. She was dressed in a new suit, one she'd gifted to herself after a job well done. As soon as she stepped out into the office, she saw Ken.

Nicky walked over to him, feeling her pules in her throat. A rare smile took over Ken's face, and he stuffed his hands in the pockets of his pants as they met up in the middle of the desks in the office.

"So, we did it," Ken said. "We have Felix in custody. He's not going anywhere. And not one person had to die."

Nicky smiled. "I'd say that's a success."

"All thanks to you," Ken said. He went quiet and rubbed a hand over his neck. "But... I want to apologize," Ken said.

"For what?" Nicky asked.

"For doubting you," Ken said. "That was wrong of me. I'm sorry."

Nicky felt her heart flutter at that. She thought he was going to leave, but he wasn't.

"I also want to say thank you," Ken said. "To you, and to the entire team. We did this. Together. You took charge, and you led us. All of us are in a better place now. It wouldn't have happened without you."

Nicky let out a breath. "Thanks," she said.

They stood there in silence for a moment. It seemed like Ken had more to say. Nicky looked up into his eyes, and the corners of her lips curled up into a smile. For a moment, they just stood there, staring at one another.

Finally, Nicky put her hand on Ken's arm. "I'm glad you're okay," she said. "And I'm glad I'm not alone here."

Ken put his hand over hers, and a smile spread across his lips. He let out a breath, and his eyes bored into hers. "Me too," he said.

A moment passed, and they stared at one another, both knowing they had something more to say. Nicky looked up at Ken, and he looked down at her. Neither one of them was sure what to do from there.

"Good job, Ken," Nicky said. "Thanks again. And now—I have a meeting alone with the chief."

"What about?"

She smiled. "I'll tell you later."

"Sounds interesting," Ken said.

Nicky nodded, and then she walked away toward the chief's office. She knocked on the door and opened it. She walked in and closed the door behind her to see Chief Franco, as always, behind a desk stacked with paperwork. The smell of books filled her nose, and she noticed that there was a new photo on the chief's desk—one of his kids and his husband, Greg. Nicky couldn't help but smile. Chief Franco was a closed off guy, and not much was known about him—especially not about his family life.

But Nicky could tell that he was happy with his life.

"Thank you for coming, Agent Lyons," the chief said. "Please take a seat."

Nicky sat down in the chair across from the chief, and Franco put his elbows on the desk and steepled his fingers. He studied Nicky for a moment.

"You know you've been one of our best agents for a long time, Lyons," the chief said. "You've always been whip-smart, driven, and quick to act. But Agent Lyons, your work here… it's blown me away."

Nicky felt her heart flutter. "Thank you, sir," she said.

"You've handled some high-profile cases now," he said. "And that job you did with Felix? That was brilliant. You knew how to handle him, and you pulled it off in the end. I have to say, I'm impressed. Not a single one of those girls had to die, and even better, the perp himself will be in jail for the rest of his life—we don't have to deal with any body bags. Not one."

Nicky felt her face warm. It really was the ideal outcome.

"I know you met Special Agents Burke and Farris," the chief continued. "That was out of my hands; with the rate of girls going missing, the FBI wanted to send an extra pair of hands out. I told them my agents would get the job done, but even I answer to someone."

Nicky nodded, remembering how incapable she'd felt when those other agents stepped in. "I understand, Chief. There was a lot of pressure, and those two have more experience than me."

"True, but you solved the case less than twenty-four hours after they showed up."

"They were still very helpful in the search for Andersen."

"I'm glad to hear it. Now… for the debriefing." He paused, glancing over a file on his desk. "As you know, Felix Andersen is in custody. We've found out a bit more about this sick little plot he was cooking up." The chief's eyes met Nicky's. "It turned out that he had this plan to have seven wives. He had planned on kidnapping one more set of twins, and then, in his mind, he had to kill one of them so it would become an uneven number. Don't ask me why he had to enact this 'twin' plot to do it; I have no idea. The guy has more than a few screws loose. Anyway, he bought the dolls from a yard sale in Rockwood—a junk sale run by Nial Prat, one of the men you apprehended. You were really on the right track with that, but Prat is only guilty of theft."

Nicky nodded. "What Andersen planned to do with these girls… it's so twisted." She shivered at the thought of those girls, back in that dark room. She could only imagine what they had seen in there.

"He's a sick man," the chief said. "But we have him. The girls are safe, and he's behind bars. Your work on this has been exemplary, Agent Lyons. And… I wanted to let you know that I'm glad to have you on my team."

Nicky felt her eyes start to water, but she held back her tears. "Thank you, sir," she said.

"You've gotten us out of one of the toughest situations we've faced yet," the chief said. "And I can't wait to see what the future has in store for you."

Nicky smiled at that, and she couldn't help feeling a little warmth in her heart. She had worked in law enforcement for a long time, and it felt good to get a compliment from the chief.

"Thank you, sir," she said.

He let out a big sigh. "That's three of the ten women off our list saved. Seven more to go. At this rate, I'm confident you'll save each and every one of those girls, or at the very least, bring closure to their families."

Nicky bit on her lip, and a ball of anxiety grew in her chest. After what had happened, she had only become more emboldened to pitch the idea of reopening Rosie's case officially to the chief, but she was still nervous to do so—nervous she would be rejected.

Nicky would love to have the strength of the FBI behind her on this, with her spearheading the case. But she also knew that Rosie's case had been cold for well over ten years, which was a lot longer than any of the girls on their current list were missing.

Still. Nicky had to try.

"Chief, I'm…" She cleared her throat as Franco eyed her. "I'm sure you heard that Andersen, he was saying some… strange stuff about my sister."

The chief was quiet for a moment. "Walker filled me in on all that, yes. He personally thinks Felix was deliberately messing with you after knowing your case from the news."

"I know, but…" Nicky took a breath. She had to be strong and firm. "I believe he could know something. Chief, I believe there's a chance my sister is still out there."

The chief was quiet for a long moment, and then he nodded. "I see."

"I know it's been a long time," Nicky said.

"A very long time."

"But I don't want to give up hope. I don't think I could live with myself if I just gave up hope."

Chief Franco sighed and looked down at his desk. She could tell he was thinking about it—really thinking about it. It was a tense moment, and Nicky's heart raced. She felt as if it were going to burst right out of her chest.

"I had a feeling this was coming," Franco said. "You want to reopen the Rosie Lyons case."

Nicky nodded. She wanted that more than anything in the world.

The chief sighed and leaned back in his chair. "Rosie Lyons, your sister, went missing thirteen years ago, outside of Nelly, West Virginia. You were the last person to see her alive. You were also the only person to see the kidnapper."

Nicky kept quiet. She didn't know where the chief was going with this.

"But here's my issue, Lyons," he said. "You told the FBI everything you knew back then. And now, you don't know anything new at all. All you have are memories, memories you relayed to them. What would be different this time? What can you do to help this case that they couldn't do thirteen years ago? Other than your wholehearted determination, of course."

"Chief," Nicky said, "I know all that. And I've personally spent hours already looking into Rosie's case. But I care more about this than any of those agents ever did. And I have a good track record now. You know I can do it if you let me."

"You know that the FBI has a big job at hand right now, right? You're already occupied with saving the women on the list. You've already saved three."

Nicky nodded. "I know, sir."

"That means we can't spend the time we'd like to on the Rosie Lyons case. But… I want to help you. After all, it's not every day that someone comes along and offers to look at a thirteen-year-old case. It's something that has to be done well." Chief Franco leaned forward, studying her. "I've been in this business for a long time, and I know what it's like to work a case that's so close to your heart. You have to have a personal stake in the outcome. And you have that, Lyons. That's why Senator Gregory chose you for this job in the first place."

For a moment, Nicky dared to feel hope. Hope that Chief Franco was going to say yes.

"But here's the thing, Lyons," Franco said. "We have seven other missing girls on that list, and all of them, statistically, have a much higher likelihood of being alive than your sister. We can't let our personal feelings get in the way of our work. I know you want to find your sister, but I don't know if I can sign off on something that would take away from our task at hand."

Nicky's throat was so tight, she felt like she couldn't breathe. He was rejecting her. He was saying no. "But… what if I can prove that Felix Andersen knows something? What if he has new information that could break the case?"

"Of course it would be a huge break in your sister's case if we found out who kidnapped her. And if Andersen knows something, we certainly want to know, too. But Lyons, that's a big if. He said too many strange things to believe that he's really on to something. He said a lot of things about your sister for no reason other than to mess with you. He was trying to get inside your head."

Nicky's skin felt cold. "But what if he was onto something? Let me talk to him again. Let me see if I can get something out of him."

The chief hesitated, then sighed.

"I'll see what I can do."

Nicky felt warm in her heart again—warm with hope and determination. "Thank you," she said. "Thank you so much, sir."

"I don't want to see you waste your energy on this," he said. "But if you can prove that Andersen has something to say, I'll let you talk to him, and we'll see about reopening the case. But don't get your hopes up. I want you to spend all your time on the seven missing girls. That's why the senator chose you."

"Yes, sir," Nicky said, standing. "Thank you, sir."

With that, she left the room. She'd hoped she'd never have to see Felix Andersen again—but she could think of no better reason to visit him in prison.

Felix Andersen.

He hadn't changed.

Nicky was sitting across the table from the man, holding his eyes and trying to keep her cool. As far as injuries went, he was healing up about as well as she was; they both had bruised and purple faces, evidence of the fight they'd gotten into.

"I'm glad you're here, Agent Lyons," he said, smiling at her.

Nicky's stomach curled with disgust. He was a vile man, and she was happy to see him in a damn prison, where he belonged. Now, his face looked so twisted, so awful, with those pale eyes that saw everything. His face looked like a Halloween mask.

"How's my favorite FBI agent?" he said.

Nicky remained quiet.

"Not very talkative today?" he taunted.

"I'll just cut to the chase, Felix," Nicky said. "I know you aren't going to help so easily, but I may be able to get something to make your... stay at this prison a bit more comfortable if you help me out."

"Oh?" Felix lifted a brow, amused. "Is this a game, Agent Lyons?"

"No, Felix, it's not a game. I want you to tell me what you know about my sister's disappearance. About the man who took her."

"Ah," he said, leaning back in his chair. "You want to know what I know."

"Yes, I do," she said.

"I don't see why I should help you, Agent Lyons. But I like seeing you come begging to me. It's a nice reversal of roles from when you were on the other side of the table. Too bad you didn't get to finish what you started back then. Don't you regret not killing me when you had the chance?"

Nicky clenched her teeth. "Felix, I'm not interested in what you think of me. I'm interested in what you know about my sister."

"For the right price, I can tell you what you want to know," Felix said.

This was how the man played. He'd already put Nicky through hell, and she wasn't going to give in to his games now. "What's the price?" she said.

Felix gave her a smug smile. "I want to see you again."

Nicky's body froze. She hadn't expected him to say that. She'd known they would talk again, but she hadn't expected him to say he wanted to see her. She could see a wicked gleam in his eyes.

"I want to know everything about you, Agent Lyons," he said. "I want to know your deepest, darkest secrets. If you have any."

"Felix, I don't have any secrets for you to know about. I'm here about my sister."

"You don't have secrets," he said, "but you have secrets. Have you figured that one out yet?"

Nicky frowned. Despite her best efforts, a shiver ran down her spine. "What are you talking about?"

"I've watched you," he said. "I've watched you grow up and become the woman you are today. I knew about you, long before... in fact, you and you sister, you were my inspiration."

Nicky's fists clenched. He was getting under her skin. Maybe Ken was right—maybe everything this guy said was just babble, lies, bullshit. She couldn't trust anything he had to say. But she still had to know.

"What do you mean, you were inspired by us?"

"Your sister, Rosie, and yourself," he said, his eyes staring into the middle distance like he was lost in some memory. "I was inspired by him, by when he took you. You ran away, leaving your poor sister behind... I became fascinated with what would drive one to do such a thing. I became fascinated with sisters, with their dynamics."

It took everything in her not to react to his words, although they burned across her skin. "Rosie and I weren't twins," was all she said.

"Weren't you? You looked so much alike, I wouldn't have been able to tell." He smiled wistfully. "Really, it was the one who took you who inspired me the most..."

149

"Who is he?" Nicky leaned forward. "What do you know?"

"I can tell you where to find him," Felix said, leaning close to her.

Nicky inched her chair backward.

Felix smiled.

"But you won't like what you find, Agent Lyons," he said. "It's not what you want. It's not what you need."

Nicky's eyes narrowed. "Why not?"

He sighed. "Because you won't be able to save your sister."

"Why?" She had to resist the urge to reach across and beat his face in again, like she did before. "What the hell do you know?!"

Suddenly, Felix shouted, "Guards! Help me! Help! This woman is assaulting me!"

Two armed guards came into the room.

"Agent Lyons is trying to kill me!" Felix shouted. "She wants to break my nose again! Help me! Help me!"

The guards looked at Nicky. "Agent Lyons?"

"He's lying!" She hadn't been about to hit him again. She just wanted answers.

"Take me back to my cell," Felix demanded.

"No," Nicky said, "no, you have to tell me what you know!"

The second Felix was out of sight, Nicky collapsed against the back of her chair, burying her face in her hands. "Holy shit," she whispered.

She'd made so much progress, gotten so many answers, and now this, this had happened. It was all going to be for nothing. Now, she'd never know what happened to her sister. She'd never know what happened.

If Felix knew something, she had to get him to tell her.

The question was—how?

NOW AVAILABLE!

ALL HE SEES
(A Nicky Lyons FBI Suspense Thriller—Book 3)

When a senator's daughter goes missing, it is a race against time as FBI Special Agent Nicky Lyons, 28, a fast-rising star in the BAU, is tasked with finding her—and with finding, per the senator's order, the top 10 abducted women most likely to still be alive. When young women disappear along the Florida coast, Nicky realizes they're being transported somewhere across the ocean. Where is their abductor bringing them—and why?

"A masterpiece of thriller and mystery."
—Books and Movie Reviews, Roberto Mattos (re Once Gone)

ALL HE SEES (A Nicky Lyons FBI Suspense Thriller—Book 3) is book #3 in a new series by #1 bestselling and critically acclaimed mystery and suspense author Blake Pierce.

Nicky Lyons, 28, a missing-persons specialist in in the FBI's Behavioral Analysis Unit, is an expert at tracking down abductees and bringing them home. The connection is personal: after Nicky's twin sister was abducted at 16, Nicky made stopping kidnappers her life's work.

But when Nicky is assigned to a new task force in south Florida dedicated to finding the recently missing, she soon realizes she's up against a serial killer more diabolical than she imagined. Her only hope at finding these girls is entering his mind and outwitting him at his own game.

Nicky and her new partner, both headstrong, don't see eye to eye, and the case opens decade-old wounds related to her sister's disappearance. Can Nicky keep her demons at bay in time to save the victims?

Nicky, haunted by the demons of her own missing sister, knows that time will be of the essence in bringing these girls home—if it is not already too late.

A page-turning and harrowing crime thriller featuring a brilliant and tortured FBI agent, the NICKY LYONS series is a riveting mystery, packed with non-stop action, suspense, twists and turns, revelations, and driven by a breakneck pace that will keep you flipping pages late into the night. Fans of Rachel Caine, Teresa Driscoll and Robert Dugoni are sure to fall in love.

Future books in the series will soon be available.

"An edge of your seat thriller in a new series that keeps you turning pages! ...So many twists, turns and red herrings... I can't wait to see what happens next."
—Reader review (Her Last Wish)

"A strong, complex story about two FBI agents trying to stop a serial killer. If you want an author to capture your attention and have you guessing, yet trying to put the pieces together, Pierce is your author!"
—Reader review (Her Last Wish)

"A typical Blake Pierce twisting, turning, roller coaster ride suspense thriller. Will have you turning the pages to the last sentence of the last chapter!!!"
—Reader review (City of Prey)

"Right from the start we have an unusual protagonist that I haven't seen done in this genre before. The action is nonstop... A very atmospheric novel that will keep you turning pages well into the wee hours."
—Reader review (City of Prey)

"Everything that I look for in a book... a great plot, interesting characters, and grabs your interest right away. The book moves along at a breakneck pace and stays that way until the end. Now on go I to book two!"
—Reader review (Girl, Alone)

Blake Pierce

Blake Pierce is the USA Today bestselling author of the RILEY PAGE mystery series, which includes seventeen books. Blake Pierce is also the author of the MACKENZIE WHITE mystery series, comprising fourteen books; of the AVERY BLACK mystery series, comprising six books; of the KERI LOCKE mystery series, comprising five books; of the MAKING OF RILEY PAIGE mystery series, comprising six books; of the KATE WISE mystery series, comprising seven books; of the CHLOE FINE psychological suspense mystery, comprising six books; of the JESSIE HUNT psychological suspense thriller series, comprising twenty six books; of the AU PAIR psychological suspense thriller series, comprising three books; of the ZOE PRIME mystery series, comprising six books; of the ADELE SHARP mystery series, comprising sixteen books, of the EUROPEAN VOYAGE cozy mystery series, comprising six books; of the LAURA FROST FBI suspense thriller, comprising eleven books; of the ELLA DARK FBI suspense thriller, comprising fourteen books (and counting); of the A YEAR IN EUROPE cozy mystery series, comprising nine books, of the AVA GOLD mystery series, comprising six books (and counting); of the RACHEL GIFT mystery series, comprising ten books (and counting); of the VALERIE LAW mystery series, comprising nine books (and counting); of the PAIGE KING mystery series, comprising eight books (and counting); of the MAY MOORE mystery series, comprising eleven books (and counting); the CORA SHIELDS mystery series, comprising five books (and counting); of the NICKY LYONS mystery series, comprising five books (and counting), and of the new CAMI LARK mystery series, comprising five books (and counting).

An avid reader and lifelong fan of the mystery and thriller genres, Blake loves to hear from you, so please feel free to visit www.blakepierceauthor.com to learn more and stay in touch.

BOOKS BY BLAKE PIERCE

CAMI LARK MYSTERY SERIES
JUST ME (Book #1)
JUST OUTSIDE (Book #2)
JUST RIGHT (Book #3)
JUST FORGET (Book #4)
JUST ONCE (Book #5)

NICKY LYONS MYSTERY SERIES
ALL MINE (Book #1)
ALL HIS (Book #2)
ALL HE SEES (Book #3)
ALL ALONE (Book #4)
ALL FOR ONE (Book #5)

CORA SHIELDS MYSTERY SERIES
UNDONE (Book #1)
UNWANTED (Book #2)
UNHINGED (Book #3)
UNSAID (Book #4)
UNGLUED (Book #5)

MAY MOORE SUSPENSE THRILLER
NEVER RUN (Book #1)
NEVER TELL (Book #2)
NEVER LIVE (Book #3)
NEVER HIDE (Book #4)
NEVER FORGIVE (Book #5)
NEVER AGAIN (Book #6)
NEVER LOOK BACK (Book #7)
NEVER FORGET (Book #8)
NEVER LET GO (Book #9)
NEVER PRETEND (Book #10)
NEVER HESITATE (Book #11)

PAIGE KING MYSTERY SERIES

THE GIRL HE PINED (Book #1)
THE GIRL HE CHOSE (Book #2)
THE GIRL HE TOOK (Book #3)
THE GIRL HE WISHED (Book #4)
THE GIRL HE CROWNED (Book #5)
THE GIRL HE WATCHED (Book #6)
THE GIRL HE WANTED (Book #7)
THE GIRL HE CLAIMED (Book #8)

VALERIE LAW MYSTERY SERIES
NO MERCY (Book #1)
NO PITY (Book #2)
NO FEAR (Book #3)
NO SLEEP (Book #4)
NO QUARTER (Book #5)
NO CHANCE (Book #6)
NO REFUGE (Book #7)
NO GRACE (Book #8)
NO ESCAPE (Book #9)

RACHEL GIFT MYSTERY SERIES
HER LAST WISH (Book #1)
HER LAST CHANCE (Book #2)
HER LAST HOPE (Book #3)
HER LAST FEAR (Book #4)
HER LAST CHOICE (Book #5)
HER LAST BREATH (Book #6)
HER LAST MISTAKE (Book #7)
HER LAST DESIRE (Book #8)
HER LAST REGRET (Book #9)
HER LAST HOUR (Book #10)

AVA GOLD MYSTERY SERIES
CITY OF PREY (Book #1)
CITY OF FEAR (Book #2)
CITY OF BONES (Book #3)
CITY OF GHOSTS (Book #4)
CITY OF DEATH (Book #5)
CITY OF VICE (Book #6)

CALAMITY (AND A DANISH) (Book #5)
MAYHEM (AND HERRING) (Book #6)

ADELE SHARP MYSTERY SERIES
LEFT TO DIE (Book #1)
LEFT TO RUN (Book #2)
LEFT TO HIDE (Book #3)
LEFT TO KILL (Book #4)
LEFT TO MURDER (Book #5)
LEFT TO ENVY (Book #6)
LEFT TO LAPSE (Book #7)
LEFT TO VANISH (Book #8)
LEFT TO HUNT (Book #9)
LEFT TO FEAR (Book #10)
LEFT TO PREY (Book #11)
LEFT TO LURE (Book #12)
LEFT TO CRAVE (Book #13)
LEFT TO LOATHE (Book #14)
LEFT TO HARM (Book #15)
LEFT TO RUIN (Book #16)

THE AU PAIR SERIES
ALMOST GONE (Book#1)
ALMOST LOST (Book #2)
ALMOST DEAD (Book #3)

ZOE PRIME MYSTERY SERIES
FACE OF DEATH (Book#1)
FACE OF MURDER (Book #2)
FACE OF FEAR (Book #3)
FACE OF MADNESS (Book #4)
FACE OF FURY (Book #5)
FACE OF DARKNESS (Book #6)

A JESSIE HUNT PSYCHOLOGICAL SUSPENSE SERIES
THE PERFECT WIFE (Book #1)
THE PERFECT BLOCK (Book #2)
THE PERFECT HOUSE (Book #3)
THE PERFECT SMILE (Book #4)
THE PERFECT LIE (Book #5)

THE PERFECT LOOK (Book #6)
THE PERFECT AFFAIR (Book #7)
THE PERFECT ALIBI (Book #8)
THE PERFECT NEIGHBOR (Book #9)
THE PERFECT DISGUISE (Book #10)
THE PERFECT SECRET (Book #11)
THE PERFECT FAÇADE (Book #12)
THE PERFECT IMPRESSION (Book #13)
THE PERFECT DECEIT (Book #14)
THE PERFECT MISTRESS (Book #15)
THE PERFECT IMAGE (Book #16)
THE PERFECT VEIL (Book #17)
THE PERFECT INDISCRETION (Book #18)
THE PERFECT RUMOR (Book #19)
THE PERFECT COUPLE (Book #20)
THE PERFECT MURDER (Book #21)
THE PERFECT HUSBAND (Book #22)
THE PERFECT SCANDAL (Book #23)
THE PERFECT MASK (Book #24)
THE PERFECT RUSE (Book #25)
THE PERFECT VENEER (Book #26)

CHLOE FINE PSYCHOLOGICAL SUSPENSE SERIES
NEXT DOOR (Book #1)
A NEIGHBOR'S LIE (Book #2)
CUL DE SAC (Book #3)
SILENT NEIGHBOR (Book #4)
HOMECOMING (Book #5)
TINTED WINDOWS (Book #6)

KATE WISE MYSTERY SERIES
IF SHE KNEW (Book #1)
IF SHE SAW (Book #2)
IF SHE RAN (Book #3)
IF SHE HID (Book #4)
IF SHE FLED (Book #5)
IF SHE FEARED (Book #6)
IF SHE HEARD (Book #7)

THE MAKING OF RILEY PAIGE SERIES

WATCHING (Book #1)
WAITING (Book #2)
LURING (Book #3)
TAKING (Book #4)
STALKING (Book #5)
KILLING (Book #6)

RILEY PAIGE MYSTERY SERIES
ONCE GONE (Book #1)
ONCE TAKEN (Book #2)
ONCE CRAVED (Book #3)
ONCE LURED (Book #4)
ONCE HUNTED (Book #5)
ONCE PINED (Book #6)
ONCE FORSAKEN (Book #7)
ONCE COLD (Book #8)
ONCE STALKED (Book #9)
ONCE LOST (Book #10)
ONCE BURIED (Book #11)
ONCE BOUND (Book #12)
ONCE TRAPPED (Book #13)
ONCE DORMANT (Book #14)
ONCE SHUNNED (Book #15)
ONCE MISSED (Book #16)
ONCE CHOSEN (Book #17)

MACKENZIE WHITE MYSTERY SERIES
BEFORE HE KILLS (Book #1)
BEFORE HE SEES (Book #2)
BEFORE HE COVETS (Book #3)
BEFORE HE TAKES (Book #4)
BEFORE HE NEEDS (Book #5)
BEFORE HE FEELS (Book #6)
BEFORE HE SINS (Book #7)
BEFORE HE HUNTS (Book #8)
BEFORE HE PREYS (Book #9)
BEFORE HE LONGS (Book #10)
BEFORE HE LAPSES (Book #11)
BEFORE HE ENVIES (Book #12)
BEFORE HE STALKS (Book #13)

BEFORE HE HARMS (Book #14)

AVERY BLACK MYSTERY SERIES
CAUSE TO KILL (Book #1)
CAUSE TO RUN (Book #2)
CAUSE TO HIDE (Book #3)
CAUSE TO FEAR (Book #4)
CAUSE TO SAVE (Book #5)
CAUSE TO DREAD (Book #6)

KERI LOCKE MYSTERY SERIES
A TRACE OF DEATH (Book #1)
A TRACE OF MURDER (Book #2)
A TRACE OF VICE (Book #3)
A TRACE OF CRIME (Book #4)
A TRACE OF HOPE (Book #5)

Lightning Source UK Ltd.
Milton Keynes UK
UKHW010253090223
416650UK00002B/400